New e for English

A1>A2

Workbook 6e

Cycle 3

Direction pédagogique

Mélanie Herment
Professeur et formatrice
Académie de Paris

AUTEURS

Laura Cursat
Professeur
Académie de Besançon

Anna Guill
Professeur et formatrice
Académie de Versailles

Pascaline Gouyette
Professeur
Académie de Paris

Sophie Rosenberger
Docteur en linguistique anglaise

Corinne Létant
Professeur
Académie de Paris

Karine Letellier
Professeur
Académie de Paris

Mark Wallace
Professeur
Académie de Paris

Liaison CM2 – 6e
Charlotte Thomas
Formatrice à l'INSPE de Paris

didier

Remerciements

L'éditeur exprime toute sa reconnaissance à Annie Coghlan pour sa relecture attentive et exigeante et ses suggestions toujours pertinentes, qui ont grandement bénéficié à l'ensemble du projet.

Édition : Virginie Soubelet, Claudine Varin

Responsable éditoriale : Catherine Laurent

Conception maquette intérieure : Anne-Danielle Naname - Adeline Calame

Conception couverture : Nicolas Piroux

Mise en page : Anne-Danielle Naname - Adeline Calame

Illustrations : Sylvie Eder, Johanna Crainmark, Pierre Botherel, Laurent Audoin, Jan Bielecki

Cartes : Johanna Crainmark

Iconographie : Julia Chiron, Maria Mora Fontanilla

Photogravure : Anne-Danielle Naname

PAPIER À BASE DE FIBRES CERTIFIÉES

éditions didier s'engagent pour l'environnement en réduisant l'empreinte carbone de leurs livres. Celle de cet exemplaire est de :
800 g éq. CO_2
Rendez-vous sur www.editionsdidier-durable.fr

© Les Éditions Didier, Paris, 2021 - ISBN: 978-2-278-10297-6 - Dépôt légal : 10297/01
Achevé d'imprimer en Italie par L.E.G.O. S.p.a. (Lavis) en avril 2021

SOMMAIRE

Fiches & activités

PROJECT 1

Welcome to English class

LESSON 1 NICE TO MEET YOU! Textbook p. 14-15

2 b. Complete the children's identity cards. Circle their cities on the maps.

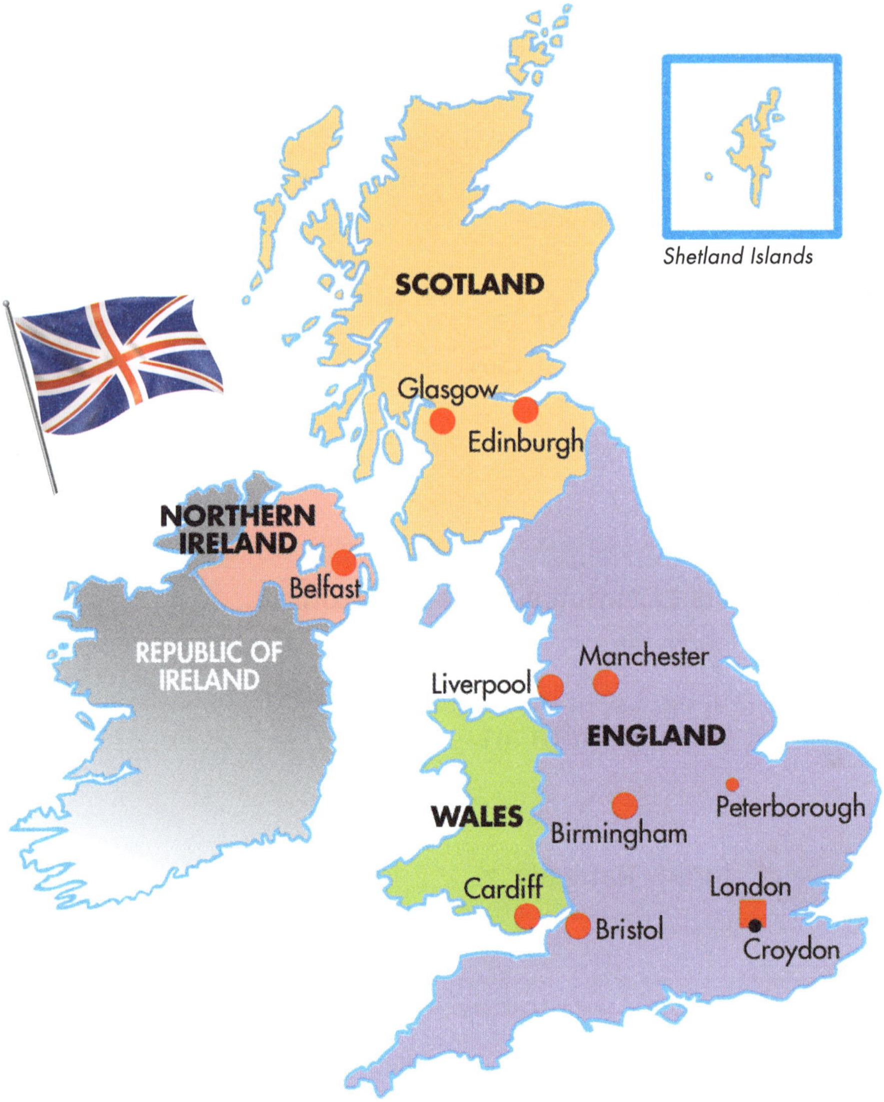

Name: Emily

Age: ....

Class: ....

Country: ....

City: ....

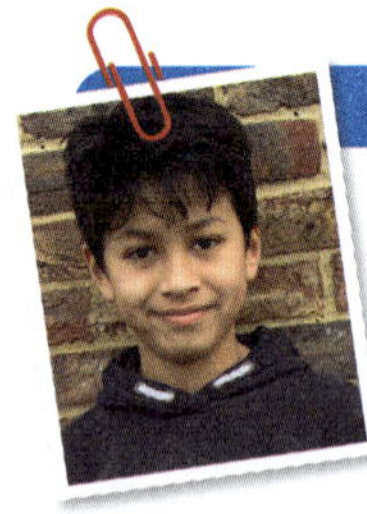

Name: ....

Age: ....

Class: ....

Country: ....

City: ....

Name: ....

Age: ....

Grade: ....

Country: ....

City: ....

Name: ....

Age: ....

Grade: ....

Country: ....

City: ....

Are you a geography expert?

a. Can you spot these countries on a world map?

The USA (The United States of America)

The UK (The United Kingdom)

Spot France too!

b. Colour them in and write their names.

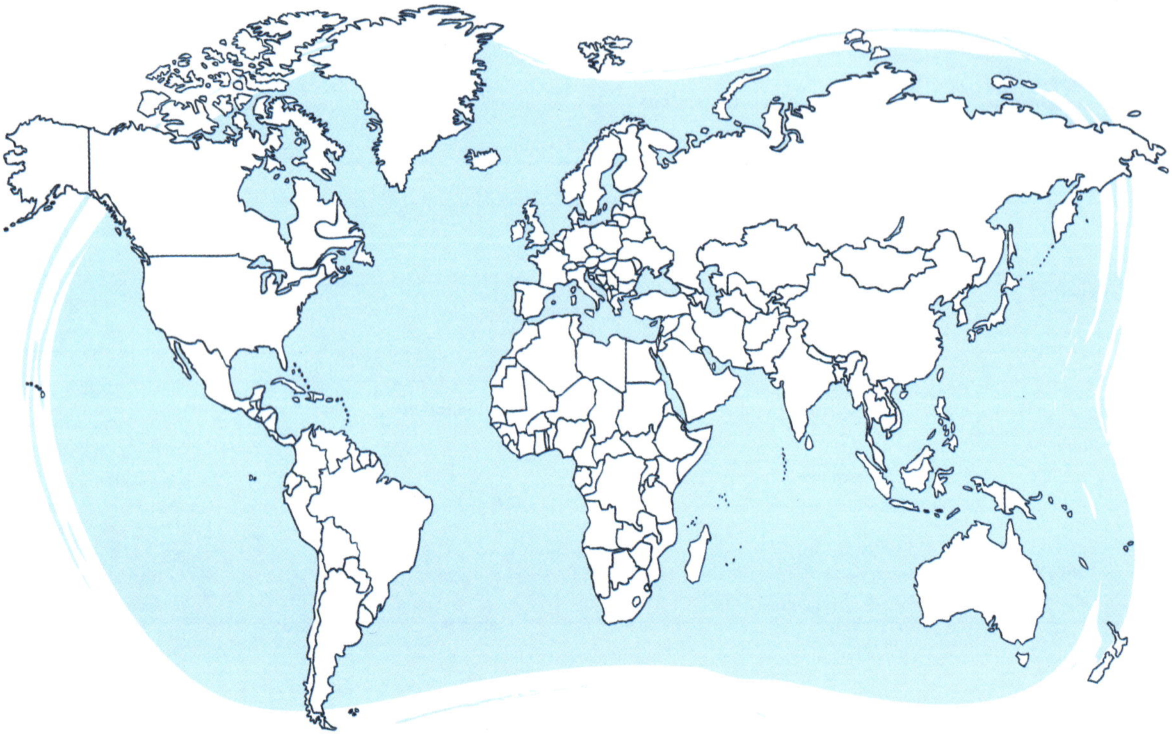

Challenge!

Connais-tu d'autres pays où l'on parle anglais ? Indique-les sur la carte.

Time to write **Complete Emily's introduction.**

Hello! My name is ....

....

....

....

....

....

....

....

....

WORDS

Fais ces exercices sans regarder ton manuel, puis vérifie tes réponses !

Textbook p. 16

AT HOME

1 ★ **Concours de calcul ! Écris le résultat de ces opérations en toutes lettres.**

2 + 7 = nine....................

16 + 8 = ...

15 + 4 = ...

10 + 20 = ...

9 x 10 = ...

30 – 8 = ...

2 ★★ ***My life in numbers!***

a. Complète cette biographie chiffrée de Harry Potter avec les nombres ci-dessous.

one | two | four | seven | eleven | one hundred and sixteen

Harry Potter in numbers

The books

.... : the number of books in the *Harry Potter* series.

Hogwarts

.... : the number of houses at Hogwarts.

.... : Dumbledore's age.

Harry Potter

Harry is .... years old when he goes to Hogwarts.

He has .... best friends and .... mortal enemy: Voldemort!

b. **À ton tour ! Écris tes réponses en toutes lettres.**

MY LIFE IN NUMBERS

Age: ....

Number of letters in my name: ....

Number of brothers and sisters: ....

Favourite number: ....

Number of pets I have: ....

3 **Complète cette fiche d'identité en utilisant les informations fournies :**

Name: ....

Surname: ....

Age: ....

City: ....

State: ....

Country: ....

The U.S.A. | Julian | Los Angeles | California | LOPEZ | 13

4 **Tu as trouvé un album de timbres chez tes grands-parents. Certains ne sont pas légendés. À toi de le faire !**

.... : région, état ou ville
.... : pays

Aide-toi :
- de ce qui est écrit sur les timbres,
- des lieux ou monuments représentés,
- des cartes pages 4 et 5.

This stamp is from

.....................................,

....

This stamp is from

.....................................,

....

This stamp is from

.....................................,

....

BE au Présent

1 ★ **Te souviens-tu d'Emily et de Noah ? Complète leurs présentations.**

Emily .... from England.
She .... 10 years old.

Hello! My name .... Noah.
I .... from the United States.
I .... in the 4th grade.

2 ★★ **Tu crées une bande dessinée, voici tes héros ! Imagine comment chacun se présente.**

Shana - 10 - Washington DC

....
....
....
....

Jamie - 11 - London

....
....
....
....

Imagine leur ennemi juré.

Conjugue 'BE' à la forme qui convient !

Dessine l'ennemi juré !

....
....
....
....
....
....
....
....

Imagine comment il ou elle se présente.

3 ★★ **Écoute et coche la forme conjuguée du verbe *BE* que tu entends.** efe6035

1. ☐ am ☐ is ☐ are
2. ☐ am ☐ is ☐ are
3. ☐ am ☐ is ☐ are
4. ☐ am ☐ is ☐ are

LESSON 2 LET'S SING! Textbook p. 19

Sing along to the music!

Time to write **Use these words to complete the lyrics.**

Use the rhymes!

Hello | Yes | Goodbye | I don't know

Stop | Say | Why | No

Hello Goodbye

You say ...., I say ....
You say .... and I say "go, go, go"
Oh no

You say ...., and I say "................, ..., ..."
.... why you say "..............................", I say "Hello, hello, hello"
I don't know why you say "Goodbye", I say "..............................."

I .... "high", you .... "low"
You say "Why?" and I say "..............................."
Oh no

You say "..............................", and I say "Hello, hello, hello"
.... why you say "Goodbye", I say "Hello, hello, hello"
I don't know .... you say "Goodbye", I say "................"

The Beatles, 1967

Build your VOCABULARY!

a. Complete the speech balloons with words from the song.

Yes	....
Stop	....
....	Hello
.... ?	I don't know.

b. Listen to the scenes from this comic book and complete it. e efe6036

WORDS

Fais ces exercices sans regarder ton manuel, puis vérifie tes réponses !

Textbook p. 20

AT HOME

1 ✱ **Allez, on joue ? Trouve les mots mêlés dans cette grille.**

A	D	A	M	X	C	L	Y	A	N
S	K	F	D	N	P	T	H	E	Y
O	M	T	G	X	M	M	C	E	W
N	T	E	O	D	O	N	Y	S	Q
G	S	R	O	B	R	G	I	Q	P
B	I	N	D	A	N	T	W	N	A
J	N	O	B	I	I	U	O	M	G
V	G	O	Y	S	N	I	G	H	T
R	N	N	E	S	G	M	O	G	A
G	A	L	I	S	T	E	N	M	C

GOODBYE
~~HEY~~
SONG
SING
LISTEN
MORNING
NIGHT
AFTERNOON

2 ✱ **On ne se salue pas de la même façon selon le moment de la journée, ou selon la personne à qui l'on s'adresse. Écris les expressions qui conviennent.**

1. ....

2. ....

3. ....

4. ....

5. ....

6. ....

Textbook p. 21

AT HOME

Les pronoms personnels

1 ✱ **Choisis les pronoms qui conviennent pour compléter ces phrases :**

1. "How are .... ?"

   ".......................... 'm fine, thanks."

2. "Are .... from England?"

   "No, ... 'm from Scotland."

3. "Who are Debbie and Chris?"

   ".......................... 're my parents."

4. "Who are The Beatles?"

   " .... 're a very famous British band from the 1960's."

2 ✱ **Choisis les pronoms qui conviennent pour compléter ces phrases :**

An interview with Paul McCartney

Do you know the Beatles? .... are one of the most successful bands in the history of modern music. Today, ... am in the company of Paul McCartney!

Hello, Paul. Nice to meet .... !

Very nice to meet .... too!

Where are .... from?

.... 'm from Liverpool, in England.

How old are .... ?

.... 'm 78 years old.

.... am a big fan of *Yesterday* and *Hey Jude*. .... are great songs!

Thank you! .... are my favourite too.

LESSON 3 ALL ABOUT ME! Textbook p. 22-23

1. Get to know Greg!

2 Take a closer look at Greg's brain!

a. Imagine examples for these categories.

b. What words are also in *your* brain? Circle them and share one word with the class.

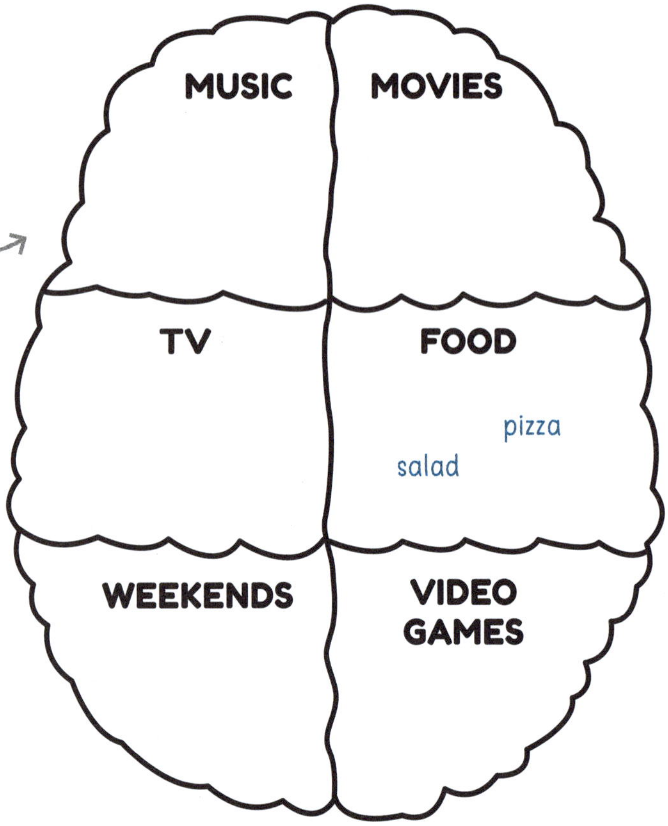

Illustration librement inspirée de *The Wimpy Kid*

2. Food, friends and music!

2 Listen to Emily and draw her brain. efe6023

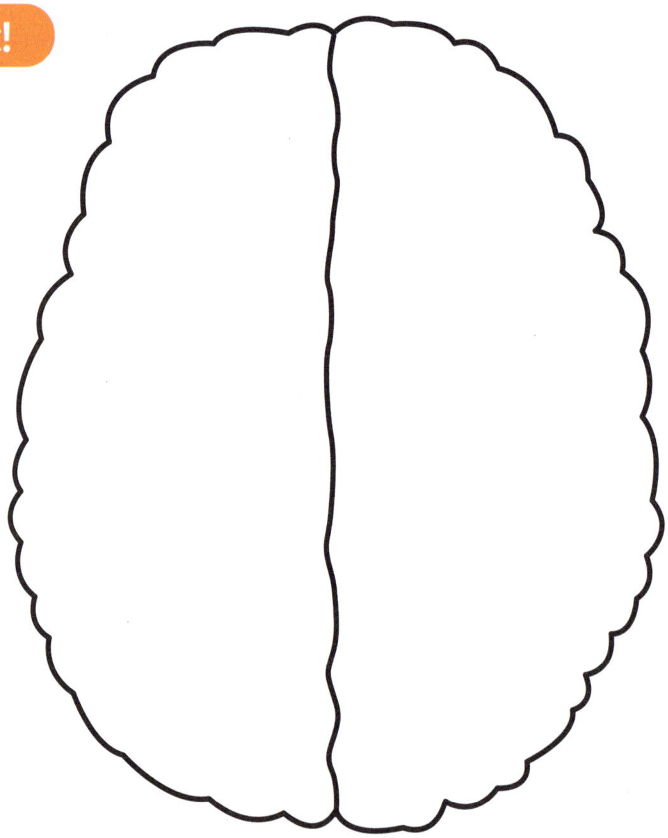

WORDS

Fais ces exercices sans regarder ton manuel, puis vérifie tes réponses !

Textbook p. 24

PROJECT 1

AT HOME

1 ✱ **Allez, on joue ? Trouve les mots mêlés dans cette grille.**

S	K	O	O	S	C	H	O	O	L
A	I	M	U	S	I	C	M	N	W
R	F	Z	O	S	N	G	O	X	S
T	P	E	T	S	E	Ç	V	G	Ç
F	O	O	D	R	M	A	I	A	S
C	L	O	O	H	A	S	E	M	P
F	R	I	E	N	D	S	S	E	O
U	U	P	N	B	O	O	K	S	R
H	O	B	B	I	E	S	N	Y	T
V	I	D	E	O	G	A	M	E	S

FOOD
MUSIC
MOVIES
FRIENDS
HOBBIES
SPORTS
VIDEOGAMES
GAMES
BOOKS
SCHOOL
ART
PETS
CINEMA

2 ✱ **Lis bien les mots de chaque liste. Qu'ont-ils en commun ? Propose un titre. Puis complète chaque liste avec un nouvel exemple.**

HELP

Food
Movies
Books
Pets

....

– snake
– dog
– cat
– hamster
– ....

....

– *E.T.*
– *Star Wars*
– *The Simpsons*
– *Pirates of the Caribbean*
– ....

....

– *Harry Potter*, by J.K. Rowling
– *Charlie and the Chocolate Factory*, by Roald Dahl
– *The Hobbit*, by J.R.R. Tolkien
– ....

....

– scones
– apple pie
– scrambled eggs
– hamburgers
– ....

✱✱ **À toi de créer une nouvelle liste !**

....

– ....
– ....
– ....
– ....
– ....

3 ✦✦ **Regarde bien ces images. Utilise-les pour trouver qui est qui sur la photo ci-dessous !**

There is... / There are...

1 **Qu'y a-t-il au menu aujourd'hui ? Complète les phrases en conjuguant le verbe *BE* correctement.**

1. There .... tomato salad and soup.
2. There .... hamburgers and pizza
3. There .... pizza and pasta.
4. There .... steak and fries.
5. There .... chocolate cookies.
6. There .... yoghurt and fruit salad.

TODAY'S MENU

Tomato salad
Soup
***
Hamburgers
Pizza
Pasta
Steak and fries
***
Yoghurt
Chocolate cookies
Fruit salad

2 **Qu'y a-t-il dans la tête de Sarah ?**

There ....

....

....

....

LESSON 4 WHAT'S IN YOUR SCHOOLBAG?
Textbook p. 26-27

1. In my schoolbag, there is...

Time to write **Label the school supplies.**

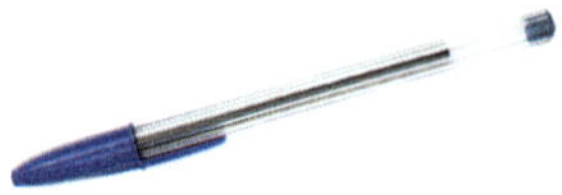

1. ....a pen..............

2. ....

3. ....

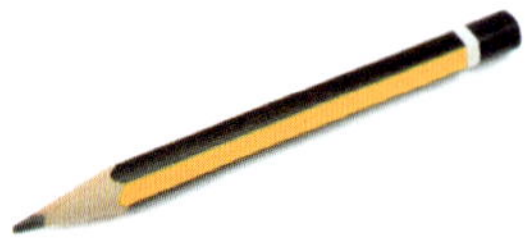

4. ....

5. ....

6. ....

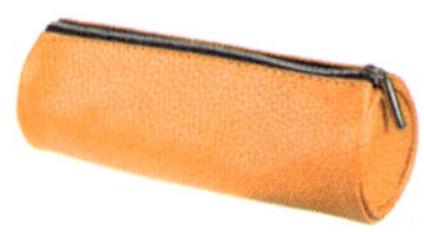

7. ....

8. ....

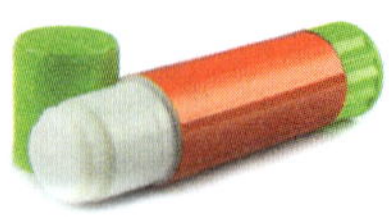

9. ....

10. ....

11. ....

12. ....

13. ....

HELP

a schoolbag / a notebook / a book / a pencil case
a pen / an ink pen / a pencil / an eraser / a pencil sharpener / highlighters /
a glue stick / a ruler / scissors

2. School supplies... Really?

School Supplies

Backpack.
Fruit snack.
Waterbottle too.
Calculator.
French Translator.
Pink eraser.
Glue.

Notebooks.
Workbooks.
Poster paper.
Pens.
Dictionary.
Stationery.
Presents for my friends.

Lunchbox.
Tube socks.
Watercolors.
Tape.
Yellow pencils.
Plastic stencils.
One for every shape.

Wristwatch.
Stopwatch.
Cell phone.
DVD.
New computer.
Motorscooter.
Giant screen T.V.

That's my list
of all I need to buy.
I never knew
a shopping list
could make my mother cry.

Kenn Nesbitt (2007)

2 **Read and listen along up to line 28.** efe6029

— Link the pictures with words from the poem.

— Add some more illustrations.

— Is it a traditional school supply list? ☐ yes ☐ no

— Highlight the "real" school supplies. What are the others?

....

Work on RHYMES!

1. **Listen to stanza 1 again.** Can you hear the rhymes? Repeat the lines.
2. **Listen to the whole poem.** Find words that rhyme with:

- too (l. 3): ....
- eraser (l. 6): ....
- pens (l. 11): ....
- lunchbox (l. 15): ....
- tape (l. 18): ....
- DVD (l. 25): ....
- computer (l. 26): ....
- cry (l. 33): ....

WORDS

Fais ces exercices sans regarder ton manuel, puis vérifie tes réponses !

Textbook p. 28

AT HOME

1 ✱ **Il y a des choses bizarres dans ces cartables !**
Barre-les et remplace-les par des fournitures scolaires adaptées aux cours.

1. notebooks – a ruler – a pizza – pencils ....
2. highlighters – a glue stick – videos – an eraser ....
3. a toy – a pencil case – a pencil sharpener – a calculator ....
4. glue – a workbook – scissors – socks ....

2 ✱ **Aujourd'hui, tu as cours d'anglais.**
De quelles fournitures vas-tu avoir besoin ? Dessine-les et légende-les.

3 ✱✱ **Te voilà en cours d'arts plastiques. Mélange les couleurs et écris-les en toutes lettres.**

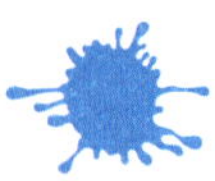 +  = blue.................... + yellow................ = green................ 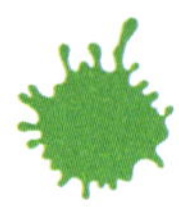

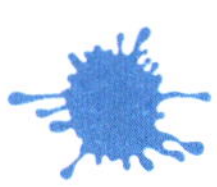 +  = ... + ... = ...

 +  = ... + ... = ...

 + 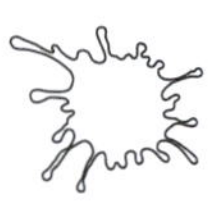 = ... + ... = ...

L'article *a* (*an*)

1 ★ **C'est ton premier cours de géographie… Ton professeur vérifie le matériel scolaire. Complète ses questions avec *a* ou *an*.**

Do you have .... ruler? .... eraser? .... notebook? .... orange highlighter? .... glue stick?

2 ★★ **Liste ces fournitures scolaires.**

N'oublie pas l'article qui convient : *a*, *an* ou ∅. Tu peux mentionner la couleur si cela te semble utile. Fais attention à l'ordre des éléments !

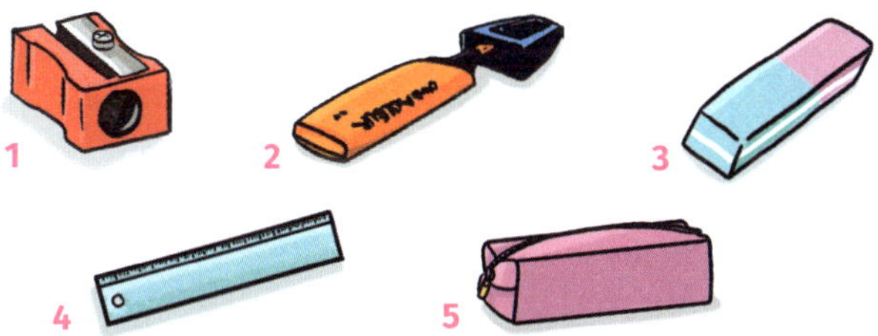

a blue ruler..........................
....
....
....
....

3 **The odd one!** IN PAIRS

★★★ **Décris ce qu'il y a dans ta trousse en ajoutant un intrus. Ton ou ta camarade saura-t-il le trouver ?**

In my pencil case, there ....
....
....
....

4 ★★★ **Mais de quoi parle-t-on ?**

On parle…

1. I love **food**!
   - ☐ de nourriture en général
   - ☐ d'un type de nourriture en particulier
2. There is **a movie** on TV.
   - ☐ d'un film en particulier
   - ☐ des films en général
3. I like **video games**.
   - ☐ des jeux vidéo en général
   - ☐ d'un jeu vidéo en particulier
4. On my bookshelf, there is **a book about Canada**.
   - ☐ d'un livre en particulier
   - ☐ des livres en général

Quiz

1 Quel âge ont les personnes qui parlent ? Entoure la bonne réponse. (efe6037)

1. 50 15
2. 34 24
3. 13 30
4. 21 20
5. 21 12

Listen up!

Guess the password!

2 Écoute bien et devine de quelle célébrité il est question. Son nom sera le mot de passe pour ton prochain cours d'anglais ! (efe6038)

I know! The password is: ....

Greetings

3 À quel moment de la journée ces personnes se parlent-elles ? Coche la bonne réponse. (efe6039)

1. ☐ matin ☐ après-midi ☐ soir ☐ nuit
2. ☐ matin ☐ après-midi ☐ soir ☐ nuit
3. ☐ matin ☐ après-midi ☐ soir ☐ nuit
4. ☐ matin ☐ après-midi ☐ soir ☐ nuit

Guess Who?

4 Reconnais-tu le personnage évoqué ? Connais-tu le livre dont il est tiré ? (efe6040)

I know! It's ....

PROJECT 2

Have a spooky Halloween

LESSON 1

1. Spooooky !

Textbook p. 32

Time to write **Create a Halloween word cloud.**

ghost

Halloween

monster

2. The perfect Halloween

Textbook p. 32

2 b. Discover more Halloween costumes.

Build your VOCABULARY!

Do you recognize these costumes?

Pour t'aider, suis les étapes indiquées p. 25.

1. ......witch..........

2. ....

3. ....

4. ....

5. ....

6. ....

7. ....

8. ....

9. ....

10. ....

11. ....

12. ....

1. **Read the words and listen to them.** efe6065

angel – fireman – pirate – witch – ghost – devil – werewolf – bat – mummy – grim reaper – skeleton – scarecrow

2. **Write the correct word under each picture.**
3. **Check with your classmates and your teacher.**
4. **Listen again and repeat the words.**
5. **Circle your favourite costumes for Halloween and tell the class!**

My favourite costume is the ....

Procède méthodiquement :

1. Commence par les mots que tu connais.
2. Appuie-toi sur la ressemblance avec le français.
3. Décompose les mots qui peuvent l'être et appuie-toi sur ce que tu comprends : *fire-man, were-wolf...*
4. Procède par élimination !

MINI TASK!

Textbook p. 33

Plan Halloween celebrations for your class! (IN GROUPS)

1. **Choose five Halloween activities you can do in class.**

– ....

– ....

– ....

– ....

– ....

2. **Write the "*do's and don'ts*" of a good classroom Halloween!**

✔ DO	✗ DON'T
- Wear a costume........................	- Don't shout!........................
- Bring	- ....
....	....
....	....
....	....

3. **Share your program with your class.**
4. **Vote for the best program!**

My favourite program is ....

LESSON 2

1. Have fun with a poem about candies!

Textbook p. 34

2 Read the poem and listen to it. e efe6053

a. Try to match some of the candies with their pictures.
- Underline the candies in the poem.
- Write the correct name under each picture.

Quand tu recopies, fais bien attention à l'ordre des lettres.

M...................
J...................

B...........................

J...................

T...................
P...................

The One Who Invented Trick or Treat

Yes, I invented "Trick or treat"
So you could fill your mouth with sweets.
Candy bars and lemon drops,
Marshmallows and Tootsie Pops,
Butterscotch and bubble gum.
Hold out your hand – they'll give you some
Chocolate kisses, Jujubes,
Sourballs and jelly beans.
Have a cake – some cookies too.
Take a couple – grab a few
Peppermint sticks and Mary Janes,
Licorice whips, and candy canes.
Slurp some soda, munch a pie,
Don't let those M&M's go by,
Chew* that toffee, munch* those treats,
Get that caramel in your teeth.
Then come see me, I'll be here –
I'm your friendly dentist, dear.

Shel Silverstein, 2011

*munch = chew = *mâcher*

...Lemon drops...

B................
G................

C..................
K..................

J..................
B..................

C....................
C....................

M..................................

WORDS

Fais ces exercices sans regarder ton manuel, puis vérifie tes réponses !

Textbook p. 38

AT HOME

Je mémorise

1 ✱ Cite 3 décorations d'Halloween.

....

....

....

2 ✱ Cite 5 costumes d'Halloween.

....

....

....

....

....

3 ✱ Cite 3 synonymes pour dire que quelque chose te fait peur.

....

....

....

4 ✱ Écoute bien cette recette. efe6066
Pour chaque ingrédient, indique la quantité nécessaire.

My Magic Potion Recipe

Ingredients

☐ spider webs	☐ cookies
☐ skeletons	☐ lollipops
☐ candy canes	☐ pumpkin

5 Dictation time! efe6067

✱✱ Écoute et écris les mots que tu entends.

1. ....
2. ....
3. ....
4. ....

6 ✱✱✱ Écoute Martin dire ce que lui et sa sœur ont dans leurs paniers d'Halloween. efe6068
Puis écris les noms des « Halloween treats » que tu as compris.

In my bucket, I have .... , ...

and ....

My sister has .... and ....

Je m'entraîne

7 ✱✱ **Choisis des mots d'Halloween et positionne-les pour former un objet ou une décoration d'Halloween.**

Exemple :

8 ✱✱ **Acrostiche : trouve un mot d'Halloween qui commence par la lettre proposée.**

G ....

H ....

O .wl...

S ....

T ....

9 ✱✱✱ **Complète le programme d'Halloween de ces petits Américains !**

1. Decorate the house with spider .... !
2. Carve a .... and make a .... !
3. Make a pumpkin .... !
4. Wear a scary .... !
5. Bring your trick-or-treat .... !
6. Go ....

HAPPY HALLOWEEN!

AT HOME

L'impératif

1 ✱ **Prépare la fête d'Halloween de la classe ! Complète cette invitation en ajoutant les verbes manquants et en les mettant à l'impératif.**

choose | watch | bring | run | come | leave | decorate

Attention :
les verbes peuvent être à la forme affirmative ou négative !

2 ✱✱ **Peux-tu aider à rédiger le règlement du champ de citrouilles ?**
Vérifie les règles suivantes et ajoute *DON'T* devant les verbes quand cela semble nécessaire.

1. .... choose a nice and big pumpkin.
2. .... run in the pumpkin patch!
3. .... eat or drink in the pumpkin patch!
4. .... have a good time!

3 ✱✱✱ **Prépare-toi à jouer à *Simon says* !**
Écris cinq ordres, puis joue avec tes camarades

Simon says... raise your hand!

1. ....
2. ....
3. ....
4. ....
5. ....

HAVE

AT HOME

1 ★ **Complète la carte de jeu à gauche. Puis crée une autre carte pour faire la suite du jeu.**

I .... a bat.

Who .... a spider?

....

....

2 ★★ **Les élèves se préparent pour la fête d'Halloween en classe. Chacun fait le point sur ce qu'il a. Conjugue *HAVE* au présent.**

1. I .... a Halloween costume.
2. Emma .... spider webs to decorate the classroom.
3. The teacher .... a big Jack o' lantern.
4. We .... candy canes and marshmallows.
5. Who .... a trick-or-treat bucket?

3 ★★★ **Remets ces mots dans le bon ordre pour reconstituer des phrases.**

Ajoute la ponctuation !

1. my trick-or-treat bucket / I / have

....

2. the jelly beans / has / Who

....

3. We / delicious cookies / have

....

4. a mummy costume / has / My / mum

....

Quiz

e efe6069

1 Écoute des phrases contenant un mot de chaque liste et identifie ce mot.

1.	☐ lollipops	☐ tootsie pops	☐ lemon drops
2.	☐ spooky	☐ cookie	☐ creepy
3.	☐ skeleton	☐ scarecrow	☐ spider
4.	☐ werewolf	☐ witch	☐ licorice
5.	☐ horrible	☐ haunted	☐ house

Listen up!

Story time

e efe6070

2 Grace et sa famille se déguisent souvent selon un thème commun. Écoute le témoignage de Grace et retrouve la photo qui l'illustre.

Guess the password!

e efe6071

3 Écoute cette énigme. La réponse sera le mot de passe pour ton prochain cours d'anglais. Entraîne-toi à le dire correctement !

I know! The password is ....
....

Let's riddle

e efe6072

4 Écoute cette nouvelle énigme. Sauras-tu la résoudre ?

I know! The answer is:
....
....

PROJECT 3 Welcome to the world of TOM GATES

LESSON 1

1. Look inside a fantastic book!

Textbook p. 44

2 Fill in Tom's identity card.

First name: ....

Surname: ....

Age: ....

Country of origin:

....

3 Who are these characters? How are they related to Tom?
Complete the boxes:

This is ....,
his ....

This is ....,
his ....

This is ....,
his ....

HELP

Derek | Delia | Mr Fullerman

HELP

teacher | sister | best friend

2. Discover Tom's world

Textbook p. 45

2 a. Fill in Tom's portrait gallery. name? | relationship to Tom?

b. What about their personalities? Choose the right adjectives.

annoying | funny | smart | grumpy | jolly and happy

Derek ....
....
....

Amy ....
....
....

Marcus ....
....
....

Delia ....
....
....

Mr Fullerman ....
....
....

Tom's grandparents ....
....
....

Build your VOCABULARY!

Choose more adjectives to describe their personalities. Complete the boxes.

nice – kind – friendly | fun – amusing | scary – frightening

cheerful – joyful – enthusiastic | nosy – indiscreet | strict

Time to write Complete the first page of Tom's diary:

Dear Diary,

Welcome to my brilliant world!

My name is ....

I .... years old and I am in Year ....

I love ....!

This is ....

She is ....!

This is ....

This is ....

We .... in a band

together: Dog ....!!!

These are my ....

They are very ....

MINI TASK!

Talk about your family (IN PAIRS)

1 List six people from your family (or an imaginary one!).

Prépare-toi à expliquer à ton/ta camarade (en anglais, bien sûr !) qui sont ces personnes par rapport à toi.

1 ....

2 ....

3 ....

4 ....

5 ....

6 ....

2 Fill in your classmate's family tree.

Pose des questions à ton/ta camarade pour savoir où placer les personnes de sa liste.

Who is Jacques?

Jacques is my grandfather on my father's side.

On my mother's side...

On my father's side...

WORDS

Fais ces exercices sans regarder ton manuel, puis vérifie tes réponses !

Textbook p. 50

Je mémorise

AT HOME

1 ★ **Reconstitue les paires !**

father	and	mother
....	and	wife
brother	and	....
son	and	....
....	and	grandmother
uncle	and	....

2 ★ **a. Écris trois adjectifs de personnalité positifs :**

☺ ....

....

....

b. Écris trois adjectifs de personnalité négatifs :

☹ ....

....

....

3 ★ **Te voilà coiffeur/se-visagiste ! Définis le type de coiffure et de couleur de ces personnes.**

long dark hair

short straight hair

short blond hair

short red hair

long curly hair

short curly hair

4 ★★ **a. Trouve l'intrus et remplace-le par un mot qui convient.**

1. classmate – ~~uncle~~ – headmaster – pupil
→ teacher
2. pupil – teacher – neighbour – classmate
→ ....
3. aunt – stepmother – schoolmate – uncle
→ ....
4. annoying – jolly – grumpy – nosy
→ ....

b. À toi de créer une liste pour tes camarades. Trouveront-ils l'intrus ?

....

5 **Dictation time!** efe6112

★★ **Listen and write the words you hear.**

1. ....
2. ....
3. ....
4. ....
5. ....

Je m'entraîne

AT HOME

6 ✱✱ **Complète les phrases avec les adjectifs qui conviennent :**

grumpy | annoying | smart | nosy

1. My neighbour is a .... old man. He's never happy.
2. She's very .... She's very good at maths and French – and she's bilingual!
3. My classmate is really .... He speaks all the time!
4. My friend's mom is so .... ! She always asks me personal questions!

7 ✱✱ **Aide Tom à rédiger quelques phrases à propos de son entourage.**

Person or relative — Personality

1. My .... are Granny Mavis and Grandad Bob. They are always ....
2. Delia is my .... She is so .... !
3. My .... is Derek. We are neighbours and he is really .... !
4. Mr Fullerman is my .... He is very ....

8 ✱✱✱ **Écoute et complète l'arbre généalogique de Martin.** efe6113

Copie les prénoms aux bons endroits.

Teresa | Peter | Karen | Nicole | James | Harold | Julie

Les déterminants possessifs

1 ✱ **Complète chaque phrase avec le déterminant possessif qui convient.**

Exemple : Tom likes to doodle. I enjoy ....his.... doodles.

1. Liz Pichon is the author of *Tom Gates*. My teacher loves .... books.
2. Amy is nice and smart! Tom is in .... class.
3. Tom, Marcus and Amy are in the same class. .... teacher is called Mr Fullerman.

2 ✱✱ **Complète les phrases avec le déterminant possessif qui convient.**

1. Tom is not here. He is at home with .... family.
2. "Is this .... pen, Pam? " "No, it's not. My pen is dark blue. "
3. These are my best friends. .... names are Liam and Sean.
4. My family and I live here. Look! This is .... house.

3 ✱✱ **Complète ces phrases.**

1. "Do you know Amy? " "Yes, ... brother is in my class. "
2. Amy and Tom go to the same school. .... name is Oakfield school.
3. This is .... teacher, Mr Fullerman. We think he is too strict!
4. My twin sister and I are excited. It's .... birthday today!

4 ✱✱✱ **Aide-toi des dessins pour compléter les phrases. Fais bien attention au possesseur.**

Exemple : Lily is 12 years old and ....her brother.... is 8 years old.

1. We live in London. .... is very nice!

2. I have new neighbours. I like to play with ....

3. My classmates and I like maths. .... is so funny!

4. My friend has two favourite objects: .... and ....

5. I have a cat. .... is Billy.

Le génitif

1 ★ **Reformule ces groupes de mots grâce au génitif.** 's ou ' ?

Exemple : Peter / his bicycle → ..... Peter's bicycle..........

1. My aunt / her children → ....

2. My brother / his phone → ....

3. The dogs / their food → ....

4. My friends / their house → ....

5. My sisters / their bedroom → ....

6. Marcus / his textbook → ....

2 ★★ **Observe l'arbre généalogique de Harry Potter et complète les phrases suivantes :**

1. James Potter is .... husband.

2. Petunia Evans is .... aunt.

3. Dudley is.................................. cousin.

4. Harry Potter is ....
and .... son.

5. Petunia is .... sister.

3 ★★★ **Remets les mots dans l'ordre pour reconstituer des phrases.**

1. Wafers / are / favourite / 's / Tom / biscuits → ....
....

2. Delia / her / 's / hates / attitude / brother → ....
....

3. doodles /'s / dislikes / Marcus / Tom → ....
....

4. student / the / favourite / Amy Porter / teachers / is / ' → ....
....

Quiz

1 **Écoute et coche la bonne réponse :** efe6114

1. My…	☐ grandfather	☐ father	☐ grandmother
2. My…	☐ mother	☐ aunt	☐ grandmother
3. My…	☐ brother	☐ stepbrother	☐ cousin
4. My…	☐ cousin	☐ sister	☐ mother
5. My…	☐ cousin	☐ father	☐ uncle

Quiz

2 **Écoute et écris la bonne réponse :** efe6115

1. ……………………………………………………
2. ……………………………………………………
3. ……………………………………………………
4. ……………………………………………………

Listen up!

Let's riddle efe6116

3 **Écoute et résous cette petite énigme !**

I know! The answer is:

……………………………………

……………………………………

Guess the password! efe6117

4 **Écoute cette nouvelle énigme. Note la réponse, ce sera le mot de passe pour le prochain cours d'anglais !**

I know! The answer is:

……………………………………………………

……………………………………………………

PROJECT 4

Christmas time with the Royal Family!

LESSON 1

Royal family, royal traditions!

Textbook p. 56

3 Listen and discover more royal traditions. efe6150
Identify the picture corresponding to each of them.

A

Tradition n° ....

B

Tradition n° ....

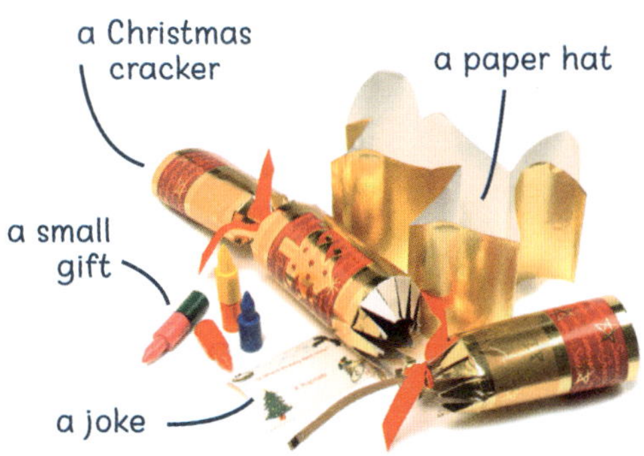

C

Tradition n° ....

D

Tradition n° ....

Time to write Complete the baubles with the traditions you have just discovered.

A

....

....

....

....

B

....

....

....

....

C

....

....

....

....

D

....

....

....

....

LESSON 2

Questions to the royal family

Textbook p. 58

Travaille sur ce texte à l'aide des consignes p. 44.

Merry Christmas

5 Redland Street
Haywards Heath
West Sussex RH17 5ST

20th December

The Duke and Duchess of Cambridge
Kensington Palace, London

Your Royal Highnesses,

My name is Harry and I am 11 years old. I live in West Sussex and I love to read about you and your family. I hope therefore that you can tell me how you spend Christmas. I spend Christmas with my family: my parents Ben and Nanette and with my sister Emily, 8, and my brother Jamie who is 6.

We usually spend Christmas at home, but sometimes we go to my grandparents' in Lancashire or to my other grandparents' in Sussex. We always put a tree up and I love to decorate it. We put all our presents under the tree. I love Christmas Eve too because we open a special box of presents: a film, chocolate, sweets and popcorn. My younger brother Jamie likes to leave a mince pie for Father Christmas and a carrot for Rudolph. We leave our stockings on our bedroom doors and we always wake up early to see what is inside them.

Do you have family traditions too? Do the children sing Christmas carols? Do you spend your Christmas in London or do you prefer going to Scotland? Does the Queen open presents too?

I hope you have a wonderful Christmas this year.

Yours sincerely,
Harry Morris

2 b. Read the first paragraph.
– Fill in Harry's identity card.

HELP
Tu recherches des personnes ou des lieux ?
Repère les mots commençant
par une majuscule !

First name: ....
Surname: ....
Age: ....
Place of residence: ....
Country: ....

– Fill in Harry's family tree.

.... — ....

.... | ....Harry.......... | ....

3 Read the second paragraph.
a. Underline all the words related to Christmas in the text.
b. Focus on Christmas traditions in Harry's family. Draw what you understand!

WORDS

Fais ces exercices sans regarder ton manuel, puis vérifie tes réponses !

Textbook p. 62

Je mémorise

1 ★ **Que fait-on à Noël ? Écris les mots correspondant aux illustrations.**

....

....

2 ★ **Des lettres se sont effacées ! Retrouve-les pour reconstituer ces phrases.**

Thank you for your lovely g _ _ t!

Merry C _ _ _ s _ _ as to you!

Have a nice hol _ _ _ _!

Do you c _ l _ _ ra _ e Christmas with your family?

3 ★ **Crée une famille royale ! Puis présente-la en donnant le titre et le prénom de chacun.**

This is .... ,

....

They have two children, a boy and a girl:

....

and ....

They live in a beautiful ....

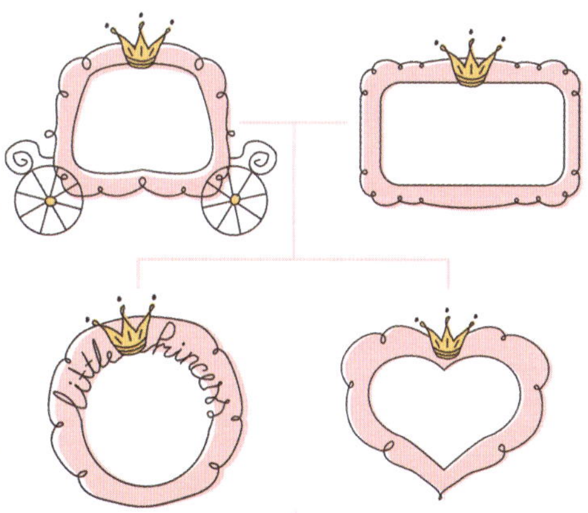

Tu peux même les dessiner !

4 ★★ **Complète ce témoignage à l'aide des verbes suivants :**

make | decorate | sing | open | celebrate

We usually .... my birthday at home.

We .... the room with balloons and flowers.

My parents .... my favourite chocolate cake.

All my friends and family .... 'Happy Birthday'.

Then finally I .... my presents!

AT HOME

5 Écoute ce poème de Noël et retrouve les mots manquants. efe6159

"I like to see the ....
I like to see the ....
I like to see the bells
I like to see the ....
And I like to see ....
Looking at ...."

6 Complète ce petit texte sur le Noël de Tom.

Every year, Tom .... a letter to Santa to describe the .... he would like to receive for .... He puts up a .... and .... it with colourful baubles and beautiful lights. In the afternoon he .... his friends and they eat ....

7 Que fait la famille Turner chaque Noël ? Regarde leur album photo et complète les phrases.

1. Mr Turner and his daughter ....
2. On Christmas day, the family ....
3. On Christmas morning, the Turners ....
4. On Christmas afternoon, ...

Le Présent simple
(formes affirmative et négative)

AT HOME

1 ★★ **Complète la lettre de Josh en conjuguant les verbes suivants :**

decorate | hang up | cook | share | eat | not/like | receive | be

Hello! My name is Josh.
Here is my ideal Christmas: I .... a huge Christmas tree with my family. On Christmas Eve, we .... our stockings by the chimney. My father .... a lovely Christmas dinner, and we all .... it together. I .... a lot of Christmas pudding because I love it but my sister .... it. How strange! I .... all my presents on Christmas Day... and I .... really happy!

2 ★★ **Depuis quelques années, les Noëls ne se passent plus de la même façon à la cour. Conjugue les verbes au Présent simple pour découvrir la situation.**

1. The Queen .... (*put up*) ten trees in Buckingham Palace. Everybody .... (*think*) it is too much.
2. No one .... (*understand*) the Christmas menu in French anymore.
3. The Royals only .... (*give*) presents to the children in their own family.
4. The Queen .... (*not/take*) the train to go to Sandringham. She .... (*drive*) there.
5. William and Kate .... (*not/send*) cards anymore.

3 ★★★ **Mr. Bean adore préparer Noël ! Raconte ce qu'il fait et quelles sont ses traditions.**

1

2

3

1 ....
2 ....
3 ....

Le Présent simple
(questions fermées)

1 ✱✱ **Connais-tu bien ton voisin ou ta voisine de classe ?**

a. Écris deux phrases à propos de ses goûts.

....

....

b. Pose-lui des questions pour voir si tu as vu juste. Prépare tes questions ci-dessous.

....

....

2 ✱✱ **Complète les questions à gauche avec les mots suivants :** do | does | is | are
Puis relie chaque question à sa réponse (à droite).

.... you celebrate your birthday with your family? •	• Not a real fan, but I like that holiday. I like to see my family.
.... Christmas on the beach fun? •	• Yes, we eat a big cake and I receive presents.
.... your family buy Christmas pudding? •	• No, my family always cooks Christmas pudding with my grandma's recipe.
.... you a Christmas fan? •	• Yes, I love to have a barbecue in the sun for Christmas!

3 ✱✱✱ **En Australie, c'est l'été au moment des fêtes de fin d'année !**
Pose des questions à un jeune Australien pour savoir comment se passent les fêtes dans son pays.

....

....

....

HELP
- plage : *beach*
- sable : *sand*
- mer : *sea*
- un barbecue : *a barbecue*
- nager : *swim*

Christmas menus

efe6160

1 Écoute Harry parler de Noël dans sa famille et concentre-toi sur ce qu'il dit à propos des repas. Coche les aliments ou plats correspondants.

Breakfast:

☐ classic English breakfast

☐ croissant

Lunch:

☐ salad and ham

☐ smoked salmon and scrambled eggs

Dinner:

☐ roast turkey

☐ roast beef

Recopie les noms des deux aliments que tu aurais le plus envie de manger !

....

Listen up!

Spot the picture

efe6161

2 Écoute Kira parler d'une tradition de Noël dans sa famille. Coche la photo qui la représente.

☐

☐

☐

Quel mot t'a permis de deviner ?

....

Guess the password!

efe6162

3 Écoute cette devinette et note la réponse. Ce sera le mot de passe pour le prochain cours d'anglais !

The password is: ....

Solve the riddle

efe6163

4 Écoute ces descriptions et devine de quoi il s'agit !

1. ☐ a stocking ☐ a palace ☐ a house
2. ☐ chocolate
   ☐ chocolate ice cream
   ☐ Christmas pudding
3. ☐ presents ☐ shoes ☐ carrots

PROJECT 5

Meet the witches

LESSON 1

1. About witches...

Textbook p. 68

2 b. *Voici deux versions du texte qui contiennent de l'aide pour comprendre. Choisis celle qui te convient le mieux.*

Version 1

Dans cet extrait, nous avons masqué les mots qui pourraient te sembler difficiles. Nous avons laissé les mots importants ou dont tu peux comprendre le sens.

Illustration : Jan Bielecki

You probably think you know **ALL** [redacted] witches. Witches [redacted] pointy black hats and [redacted] black cloaks. They [redacted] the night sky on broomsticks. Their cats are [redacted] black. [...] Right?

How to Avoid Witches, Kay Woodward & Roald Dahl, 2020

1. **Lis cette version du texte et souligne :**
   - les mots que tu connais ;
   - les répétitions – elles indiquent que l'information répétée est importante.
2. **Aide-toi du dessin pour comprendre.**
   → Fais des flèches pour relier les mots du texte à l'illustration.
3. **Utilise ce que tu as compris** pour deviner le sens des mots masqués.
4. **Discutes-en avec un camarade,** puis prépare-toi à en parler à la classe.

Version 2

Autour de cet extrait, tu trouveras des aides pour comprendre.
Ne t'inquiète pas si tu ne peux pas répondre à toutes les questions, l'essentiel est de comprendre le sens général du texte.

Qui est *you* à ton avis ?

....

Cet adjectif qualifie le mot *hats*. Appuie-toi sur sa ressemblance avec le français et sur le dessin pour deviner son sens.

....

Illustration : Jan Bielecki

You probably think you know **ALL** about witches. Witches wear pointy black hats and billowing* black cloaks. They soar through the night sky on broomsticks. Their cats are always black. (...) Right?

How to Avoid Witches, Kay Woodward & Roald Dahl, 2020

*qui volent au vent

À qui renvoie ce déterminant possessif ? (À qui sont les chats ?)

....

....

Écoute à nouveau la version lue. D'après l'intonation, à qui cette question semble-t-elle s'adresser ? À ton avis, que veut savoir le narrateur ? efe6200

....

....

....

....

....

Appuie-toi sur le dessin et sur la structure de la phrase (*and*) pour deviner à quel type de chose renvoie le mot *cloaks*.

....

Time to write **Label this picture with what you know about witches.**
Add adjectives to give more details.

....

a scary witch

a .... cloak

....

....

MINI TASK!

Textbook p. 69

Wizard wanted!

1. Before completing your poster, improve your vocabulary!

Build your VOCABULARY!

Write the words corresponding to the pictures.

....

....

....

....

....

....

....

....

....

....

....

Procède par élimination :

1. Commence par les mots que tu connais.
2. Recherche les mots au pluriel et place-les sous les photos représentant deux éléments... Attention, il y a un petit piège !
3. Appuie-toi sur la ressemblance de certains mots avec le français. Ils n'ont pas forcément le même sens, mais peuvent être de bons indices !

HELP

- a tie
- a coat
- trousers
- a shirt
- boots
- a magic wand
- a robe
- shoes
- a sweater (US)/ a jumper (UK)

WANTED

DANGEROUS WIZARD

Name: ....

How to recognize him: ....

....

....

....

....

....

....

....

If you see him, do NOT approach him. Call the Ministry of Magic immediately.

2. Complete this poster with information about your dangerous wizard.

Draco Malfoy

Gellert Grindelwald

Professor Severus Snape

Pense aux vêtements et accessoires pour le décrire. N'oublie pas de préciser leur couleur !

LESSON 2

1. Learn how to identify witches

HELP

Tu peux légender ton poster avec quelques mots utiles : cela pourra t'aider au moment de le présenter.

→ **WORDS**, manuel p. 74

3 **Draw a police sketch of a witch.**
Then present it to the other detectives in your class.

WORDS

Fais ces exercices sans regarder ton manuel, puis vérifie tes réponses !

Textbook p. 74

AT HOME

Je mémorise

1 ✱ **Barre l'intrus dans chaque liste. Puis propose un mot qui conviendrait mieux pour compléter la liste.**

1. dress – cloak – hat – cat → ....
2. trousers – nose – shirt – gloves → ....
3. fingers – skirt – teeth – hair → ....

2 ✱ **Trouve le plus de mots possibles pour légender cette illustration :**

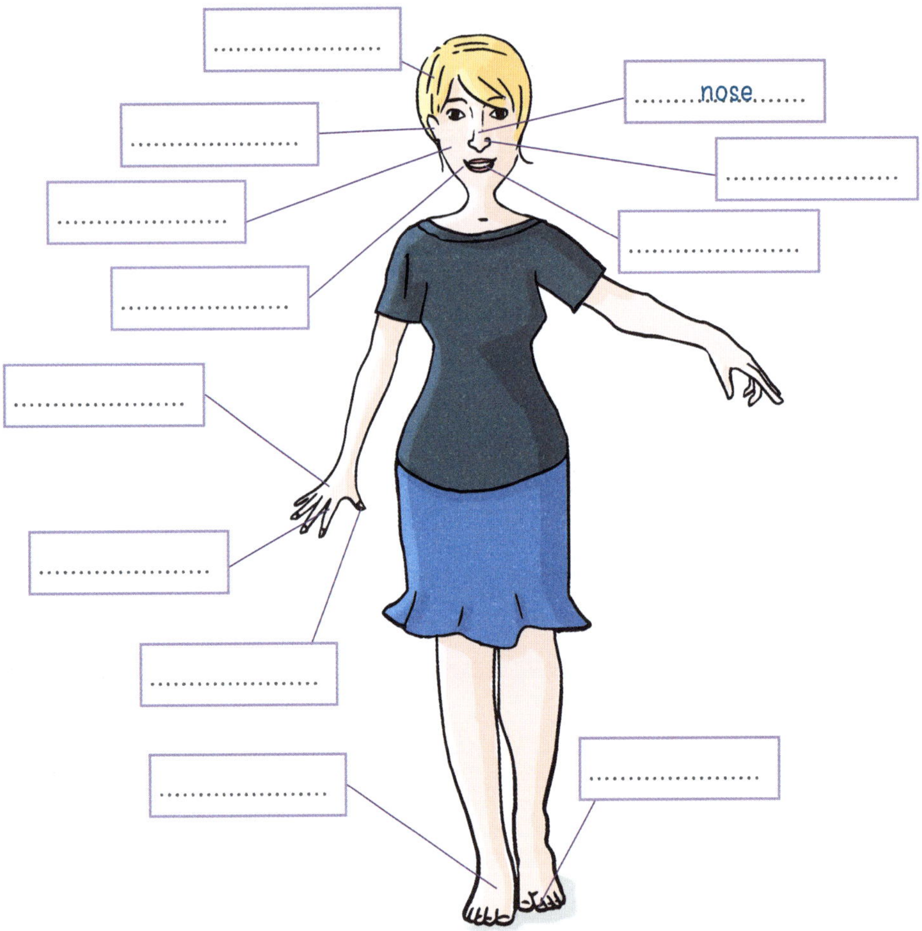

3 ✱✱ **Retrouve les adjectifs contraires et recopie-les ci-dessous.**

fat – curly – small – mean – ~~young~~ – nice – ~~old~~ – thin – straight – long – short – big

old	≠	young	....	≠	....
....	≠	....	....	≠	....
....	≠	....	....	≠	....

AT HOME

4 ★ **a. Pour chaque personnage de la saga *Harry Potter*, choisis un adjectif de personnalité et un adjectif de description physique :**

Lord Voldemort

....

....

Professor Dumbledore

....

....

Hermione Granger

....

....

Harry Potter

....

....

b. Utilise les adjectifs que tu as choisis pour compléter ces phrases :

1. Lord Voldemort is ....
2. Professor Dumbledore ....
3. Harry ....
4. Hermione ....

Personality
- intelligent
- courageous
- horrible
- kind
- scary

Physical description
- old
- young
- ugly
- bald

5 ★★ **Ton camarade est terrorisé par la sorcière qu'il vient de croiser dans le couloir du collège. Aide-le à écrire la description qu'il doit remettre au principal.**

I think this woman is a .... because she is wearing a long .... and a .... hat.
Her hair is .... She has a .... nose with large .... She is so .... !

6 ★★★ **Crée un nouveau personnage pour un film de sorcières! Dessine-le et rédige un texte pour le décrire.**

Choisis un nom pour ton personnage !

Textbook p. 76-77

AT HOME

Les adjectifs

1 ★ **a. Légende l'illustration en utilisant les noms et adjectifs fournis.**

broomstick: old | *hat:* pointy, black | *cloak:* long, black | *hair:* long, grey

Attention au choix du déterminant : *a* ou *an* ?
***a** witch* → ***an** ugly witch*
son consonne — son voyelle

....

....

....

....

★★ **b. Rédige ensuite une description de cette sorcière :**

This witch has

2 ★★ **Pour rendre ton récit plus captivant, réécris ces phrases en ajoutant les adjectifs proposés.**

Attention au déterminant ! ***a*** ou ***an*** ?

1. My neighbour is a **witch**. (*frightening*) ....
2. During the day, she looks like a **person**. (*ordinary*) ....
....
3. But at night, she has a **face**, a **nose** and **fingers**. (*scary, long, hooked*) ....
....
4. She wears a **dress** and she is really scary. (*black, old*) ....
....

3 ★★★ **Un témoin a croisé une sorcière dans le quartier.** Réécris son témoignage en apportant des précisions.

She wears a cloak. She has hair. She has shoes. She has gloves. She has nostrils.

....

....

....

Les questions

1 ★ **Associe chaque pronom interrogatif avec le groupe de mots qui convient.**

where

what

why

who

? The Grand High Witch

? In an ordinary house

? A magic potion

? Because she wants to turn all the children into mice.

2 ★★ **Tu surprends une conversation entre sorcières, mais tu n'as pas tout entendu. Essaie de retrouver leur conversation !**

Pixie: .... ?

Jinx: Yes, I do. I have a black cat.

Pixie: .... ?

Jinx: His name is Salem.

Pixie: Perfect! The cat can help.

.... ?

Jinx: My favourite spell is Abracadabra.

Pixie: .... ?

Jinx: My favourite holiday is Halloween.

Pixie: Me too! I like to dress as a witch.

Jinx: .... ?

Pixie: I always go to Flat Witch Island on holiday.

Jinx and Pixie: Ha ha ha!!

3 ★★★ **Tout en faisant mijoter une potion magique, les sorcières s'interrogent à ton propos : qui es-tu vraiment ? Imagine leurs questions.**

..Does he/she have a cat?..

....

....

....

....

Quiz

1 ★ Écoute et entoure le mot que tu entends dans chaque phrase. efe6213

1. a room – a broom – a groom
2. the witch's rat - the witch's cat – the witch's bat
3. a shirt – a skirt – a tee shirt
4. potatoes – elbows – toes

Listen up!

Guess the password!

2 ★ Écoute bien ce petit poème. Quelle fête est mentionnée ? efe6214

Note le nom de cette fête ci-dessous, ce sera le mot de passe pour le prochain cours d'anglais !

The password is: ....

Spot the witch

3 ★★ Écoute et identifie la sorcière dont on parle. efe6215

☐ **Maleficent**
Sleeping Beauty

☐ **The White Witch**
The Chronicles of Narnia

Guessing game

4 ★★★ Écoute Debbie parler du film *The Witches*. Qui est son personnage préféré ? efe6216

Her favourite character is ....

PROJECT 6

California Kids

LESSON 1

2. Eugene's California Top 3

Textbook p. 81

Time to write **Use the activities Eugene likes to decorate a board for him!**

Eugene's board

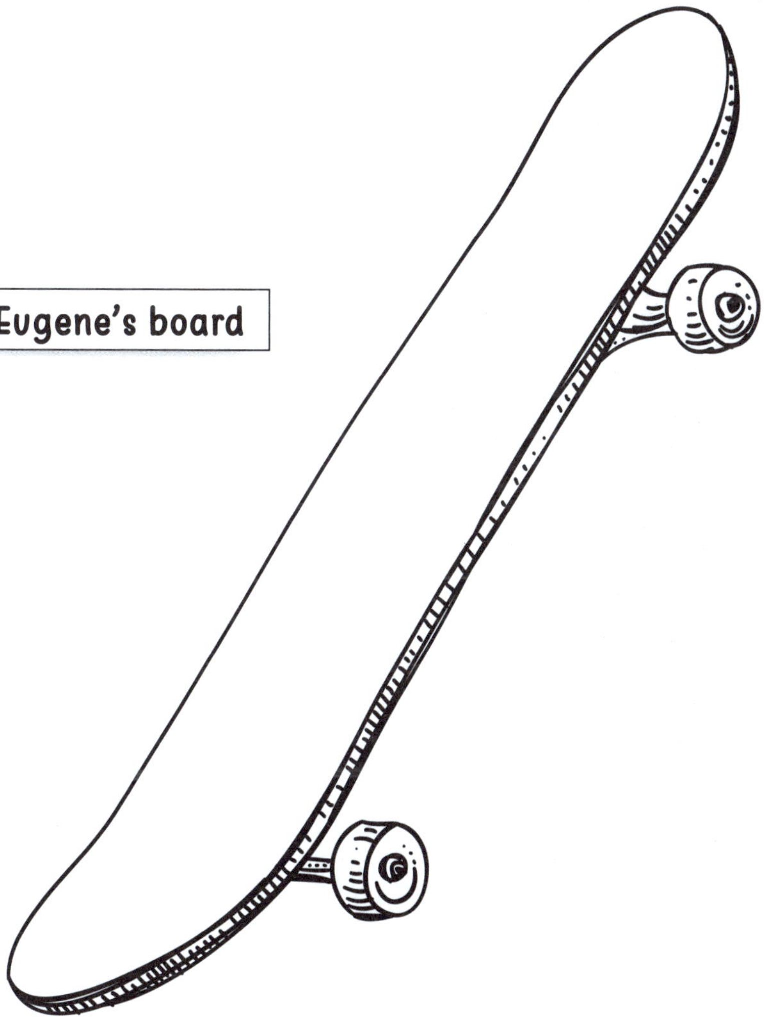

HELP

You can use:

drawings	words	phrases	sentences
	Surf	Surfer GIRL	Ride the wave

MINI TASK !

Textbook p. 81

Decorate your own board!

My board

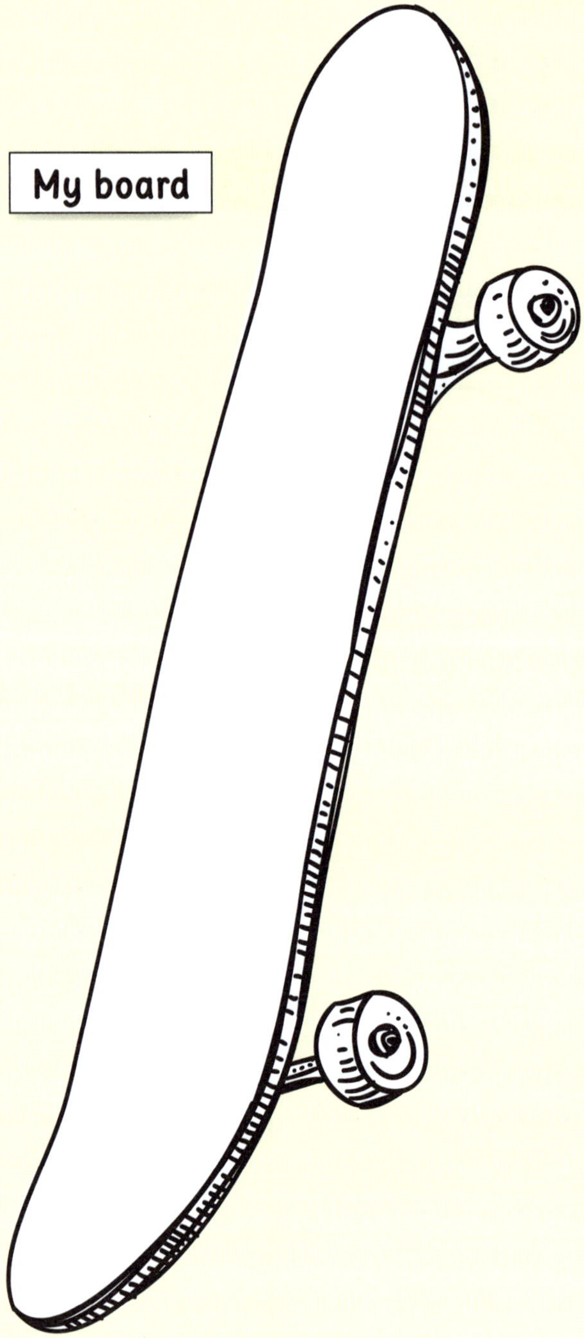

HELP

You can use:

drawings	words	phrases	sentences
	Surf	Surfer GIRL	Ride the wave

1. A day in the life of Sky

Textbook p. 82

1 **Look at the drawing. Imagine all you can about:**

Sky's favourite people | Sky's favourite activities

2 a. **Watch part 1.** Were you right? Complete or correct your notes above.

b. **Complete Sky's timetable:**

Before school	
	SCHOOL
After school	
On the weekend	

Time to write Use what you know to add speech balloons to Sky's "Draw my life".

Ajoute autant de bulles que tu veux !

WORDS

Fais ces exercices sans regarder ton manuel, puis vérifie tes réponses !

Textbook p. 86

AT HOME

Je mémorise

1 ★ **Associe chaque passe-temps de ce garçon californien avec une autre activité qu'il aime probablement.**

If he likes...	then he also probably likes...
surfing •	• going to the arcade
singing •	• skateboarding
playing video games •	• doing jujitsu
doing karate •	• dancing

2 ★ **À quelle fréquence fais-tu les activités suivantes ? Classe-les de la moins fréquente à la plus fréquente.**

talk with friends | friends stay over at my house | barbecue with friends | meet up with friends somewhere | go over to my friend's house

....

....

....

3 ★★ **Complète chaque phrase avec l'indication de temps qui convient.**

every morning | during the week | every day after school | on the weekend

Utilise chaque indication une seule fois !

1. I have cereal and orange juice .... for breakfast.
2. I like going to my friend's house .... and playing games all day!
3. I do my homework .... Then, I can play with friends outside.
4. I go to sleep early ...., but much later on the weekend.

4 ★★★ **Écoute cette jeune Californienne parler de ses activités préférées. Décore son skate en illustrant ce qu'elle aime faire.** efe6259

AT HOME

5 ✱ **Voici le profil qui apparaît sur le blog d'un jeune californien. Complète-le avec ses passions, qui sont toutes mélangées ici :**

skateboarding | surfing | video games | karate

ABOUT ME

I love going fast and jumping high, so my favorite hobby is .... But, when the weather is good, I like .... at the beach. If it rains, I go inside and play online .... with my friends. On the weekend, I go to the martial arts *dojo*, so I can do .... That's me!

6 ✱✱ **Tu vis en Californie ! Décris ce que tu aimes faire en utilisant les éléments ci-dessous :**

– meet up with my friends • have barbecues • play video games • play sports • ...
– at school • at the park • at my house/their houses • at the beach • ...

→ I like meeting up with my friends at the beach. ....

....

....

....

7 ✱✱✱ **Quelles sont tes habitudes ? Choisis trois indications de temps et écris trois phrases pour parler de ce que tu fais – ou pas !** ☺

every day | on the weekend | always | after school | sometimes | never | often

→ I read comic books and novels after school.

....

....

....

8 ✱✱✱ **Écoute cette interview d'un jeune Californien. Dessine sa vie et ajoute des légendes !** 🔊 e efe6260

....

....

AT HOME

Le nom en V + -ing (1)

1 ✱ **C'est le week-end ! Qu'aimes-tu faire ? Transforme le verbe proposé sous chaque image pour nommer l'activité qui y est représentée.**

surf → ....

skate → ....

dance → ....

play → .... video games

sing → ....

read → ....

2 ✱✱ **Regarde ce skate et écris quelques phrases pour dire ce que son ou sa propriétaire aime faire.**

....

....

3 ✱✱ **Écoute cette jeune Californienne parler de ce qu'elle aime faire ou pas, et complète ce tableau.** e efe6261

....	....	....
....	....	....
....	....	....

4 ✱✱ ***Dear Diary...*** **Écris la première page de ton journal intime. Raconte ce que tu aimes faire.**

Les adverbes de fréquence

1 ✱ **Place chaque adverbe sous le symbole auquel il correspond. Puis vérifie tes réponses dans ton manuel.** sometimes | always | often | never | usually

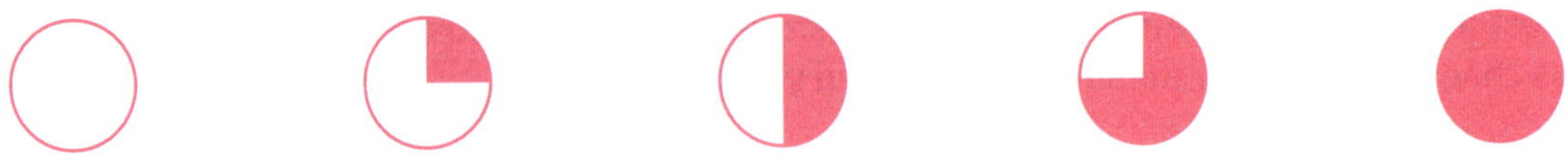

....

2 ✱ **Relie les débuts de phrases à gauche avec leur suite logique à droite pour parler du style de vie californien.**

Sometimes, we stay inside and... •	• spend a sunny day inside.
In the morning, we usually... •	• play sports.
To stay active, we often... •	• play video games.
My friends and I never... •	• eat a healthy breakfast.

3 ✱✱ **Ajoute un adverbe de fréquence pour que ces phrases correspondent à ta propre vie.**

1. I am happy. → ....
2. I am hungry at 11.30. → ....
3. I clean my room. → ....
4. I cook dinner for my family. → ....
5. I take the bus to go to school. → ....

4 ✱✱ **Complète ces phrases avec un adverbe de fréquence.** usually | often | never | sometimes

1. Kai surfs every morning. He .... sleeps past 9 AM!
2. Sky goes surfing when it is sunny, and it is .... sunny in California.
3. Sky's activities depends on the weather. She .... goes to the skatepark, and other times to the beach.
4. Sky .... teaches her brother skateboard techniques. They skate together every weekend!

5 ✱✱✱ **Et toi ? Regarde ces illustrations et écris 4 phrases pour dire ce que tu fais (ou pas !) et à quelle fréquence.**

→ *I sometimes go camping with my family on the weekend.*

1. ....
2. ....
3. ....
4. ....

Quiz

1 Écoute ces jeunes parler de leurs activités et coche les mots que tu as entendus. efe6262

1. ☐ stay ☐ play ☐ skate
2. ☐ skating ☐ surfing ☐ singing
3. ☐ karate ☐ sports ☐ skateboard
4. ☐ dislike ☐ like ☐ really like

Listen up!

Story time

2 Écoute Aaron raconter ce qu'il fait le week-end. Trace son itinéraire sur la carte de son quartier de Venice, en Californie. efe6263

Puzzle Time

3 Écris les mots que tu entends en plaçant une lettre sur chaque pointillé. Si tu les as bien orthographiés, tu devrais trouver le mot mystère ! efe6264

… … … … …

… … … … … … … …

… … … … … …

… … … … … … …

Le mot mystère est : … … … …

Guess the password!

4 Écoute cette énigme. La réponse sera le mot de passe pour ton prochain cours d'anglais. Entraîne-toi à le dire correctement ! efe6265

I know! The password is:
....

PROJECT 7 Visit London with Paddington

LESSON 1

2. Where is Paddington?

Textbook p. 92

1. b. Write the names of monuments 1 to 8 in your Guide to London below.
2. b. Listen and add information about monuments 1 to 4: **What is it?** **Where is it?** e efe6302
3. IN PAIRS Complete the information about monuments 5 to 8. Use the map in your textbook on p. 93.

Guide to London

Top places to see!

1 ..Buckingham Palace..........................

What is it?

The residence of the British monarchs.

This is where .... lives!

Where is it?

It is .... St James's Park and Hyde Park.

2 ....

What is it?

It is a ....with a very impressive dome.

Where is it?

It is .... Shakespeare's Globe Theatre and not far from the Tower of London.

3 ....

What is it?

It is a very old .... and fortress.
Today, it is a museum where you can see the Crown Jewels!

Where is it?

It is .... Tower Bridge and the River Thames.

4 ....

What is it?

It is a huge tower with a famous ....

Where is it?

It is .... the Houses of Parliament.

5 ....

What is it?

It is a reconstruction of the theatre built in 1559 by William Shakespeare. You can go and see a play there!

Where is it?

It is located .... the south bank of the River Thames.

6 ....

What is it?

It is a giant observation wheel. It offers an amazing view of the city.

Where is it?

It is situated .... the banks of the River Thames, ... the Houses of Parliament.

7 ....

What is it?

It is a round public space and a popular meeting place.
It is famous for its statue of Eros and its giant advertising screens.

Where is it?

It is .... the heart of the city.

8 ....

What is it?

It is an amazing ...., with 20 000 animals.
It is one of the top 10 family attractions in London.

Where is it? It is located .... Regent's Park.

LESSON 2

Textbook p. 94

Any suggestions?

3 **Read the other tweets to identify people's favourite places.**

> **1. Repère d'abord les noms de lieux.**
> Ils commencent par une majuscule (même s'ils ne sont pas en début de phrase) et peuvent être précédés d'une préposition de lieu.
> → Tu peux les souligner en **rouge**.

4:02 PM. • 26 sept. 2018 #Paddington London ooo **Follow**

Reporte ici le numéro de la photo concernée.

Paddington @paddingtonbear	**I am planning a day out tomorrow and I am looking for some suggestions for where to go. Do you have any favourite places in London?**	
Alice G.	What about a trip on the River Thames?	......
Chester	Changing of the Guard at Buckingham Palace. You'll love the soldiers' hats.	......
Stanley P.	How about visiting the Shard? It's amazing! You can get a panoramic view of the city of London.	......
Thomas the Man	Tower Bridge is great! They have glass floors and you can look down from way above to see the river and the boats. And you can wave at people on the bridge.	......
Mary-Ann	I suggest visiting the Lyceum Theatre. The greatest stage musical in the world, *The Lion King*, is playing there. If you can't get tickets, try another theatre nearby: there are 39 in the West End!	......
Lily	Covent Garden Market: you can shop & you can probably get a marmalade sandwich there too.	......
Paddington	It's time to start making my way home for tea. Thank you for your London adventure suggestions. Here are some pictures of my favourite places!	
Mary-Ann	Thanks for sharing your day in photos with us, Paddington!	

Compte Twitter de Paddington, sept. 2018

> **2. Essaie de comprendre les informations qui concernent ces lieux.**
> - Cherche des correspondances entre les photos p. 71 et les tweets.
> - Concentre-toi sur les mots que tu connais ou qui sont proches du français.
>
>   → Tu peux les souligner en **bleu**.
> - Fais appel à ton bon sens : que serait-il logique de faire dans chaque lieu ?

What about you?

Draw a ♥ next to your favourite suggestion. Explain why it is your favourite.

It is my favourite because you can ....

....

....

Time to write Help Paddington complete his photo album.

MY DAY OUT IN LONDON

1

....

Loved it! You can ....

....

Tower Bridge

It's impressive! From the bridge, you can ....

....

....

2

3

....

So cool... but a bit scary! You can

....

....

....

4

....

Amazing! You can ....

....

....

....

You can ....

....

....

5

6

....

Great place! You can ....

....

....

....

....

HELP

- enjoy a panoramic view of the city
- buy food and souvenirs
- watch a show or a musical
- see London's famous sites from the river
- visit...
- see the Changing of the Guard
- take pictures
- see the river through the glass floor

WORDS

Fais ces exercices sans regarder ton manuel, puis vérifie tes réponses !

Textbook p. 98

Je mémorise

AT HOME

1 ✱ **Écris les noms des lieux.**

1. ....
2. ....
3. ....
4. ....

5. ....

2 ✱ **Écris la préposition de lieu correspondant à chaque illustration.**

1. ....
2. ....
3. ....

4. ....
5. ....
6. ....

3 ✱ **Cite des activités pouvant se faire…**

1. Dans une ville : ....
2. Dans un parc : ....
3. Dans un musée : ....

4 **Dictation time!** efe6312

✱✱ **Écoute ces noms d'activités et écris-les en faisant attention à l'orthographe.**

1. ....
2. ....
3. ....
4. ....
5. ....
6. ....

AT HOME

5 ✱✱ **Maintenant que tu connais Londres sur le bout des doigts, dis si les affirmations suivantes sont vraies ou fausses (en ce cas, corrige-les !).**

Aide-toi de la carte de Londres dans ton manuel p. 93.

1. Shakespeare's Globe Theatre is situated on the south bank of the River Thames.
☐ right ☐ wrong ....

2. Hyde Park is between Buckingham Palace and Westminster Abbey.
☐ right ☐ wrong ....

3. London Zoo is located next to Hyde Park.
☐ right ☐ wrong ....

4. The London Eye is opposite the Houses of Parliament.
☐ right ☐ wrong ....

5. The Shard is near Piccadilly Circus.
☐ right ☐ wrong ....

6 **Dictation time!** e efe6313

✱✱ **a. Écoute ces noms de lieux dans Londres et écris-les, en faisant attention à l'orthographe.**

1. .... 4. ....
2. .... 5. ....
3. .... 6. ....

b. Entraîne-toi à les répéter.

c. Essaie de les retrouver sur le plan de Londres dans ton manuel p. 93.

7 ✱✱✱ **La marmelade a encore frappé...**
Paddington a reçu une invitation, mais certains mots sont maintenant peu lisibles. Aide-le à reconstituer le message !

Dear Paddington,

What .... visiting London with me on Saturday?

In the morning, we can .... on the river

and .... of the city from the boat.

For lunch, we can .... in Hyde Park and enjoy the nice weather.

Then maybe we can .... I need to buy a present for my mother!

In the evening, how about .... ? I really want to see *The Lion King*!

I hope you can come.

Love,
Jonathan

GRAMMAR

Textbook p. 100-101

AT HOME

CAN

1 ★ **"*Can*" ou "*can't*"? Complète les paroles de ces personnages de dessins animés britanniques.**

The goldfish from
Creature Comforts

I .... walk
and I .... fly,
but I .... swim.

Shaun the Sheep

I .... fly and I
.... visit the universe.

Gromit

I .... speak, but the expressions on my face speak just as well as words! I have very good ideas and
I .... easily solve puzzles.
I .... also help my animal friends on the farm.

2 ★★ **Paddington est au musée. Écris ce qu'il est autorisé à faire ou non.**

1. ....
2. ....
3. ....
4. ....

3 ★★★ **a. Écoute Joseph et coche ce qu'il sait faire ✓ ou pas ✗.** efe6314

b. Rédige maintenant ce que tu as compris.

Joseph ....
....
....
....

Le nom en V + -*ing* (2)

1 ✱ **Paddington a du mal avec l'ordinateur ! Il a oublié la ponctuation et la touche espace. Aide-le à réécrire ses messages correctement.**

N'oublie pas les majuscules !

1. whataboutcomingfortea

....

2. howaboutbringingyourdeliciousmarmalade

....

3. thankyouforwritingyourlovelyletter

....

2 ✱✱ **a. Transforme ces verbes en noms en ajoutant la terminaison -*ing*.**

Attention à l'orthographe !

cross .... smoke .... park ....

eat .... drink ....

b. Complète ces panneaux avec les noms que tu viens de créer.

3 ✱✱ **Sois aussi poli que Paddington !**
Écris un message de remerciement aux personnes qui t'ont aidé(e).

Exemple : Thank you for watering my plants!

HELP

- feed the dog
- help me with my homework
- help me cross the street

① 

② 

③ 

1. ....
2. ....
3. ....

4 ✱✱✱ **À partir des verbes suivants ou de tes propres idées, suggère deux activités à faire après l'école à un(e) camarade.**

N'oublie pas la terminaison -*ing*. Attention à l'orthographe !

go | play | watch | make something | ...

1. What about ....?
2. ....

Listen up!

Draw the missing picture!

1 Écoute Liza citer ses quatre activités préférées à Londres. Laquelle n'est pas illustrée ci-dessous ? À toi de la dessiner !

efe6315

1

2

3

Question time!

2 Un ami te propose des activités. Laquelle préfères-tu ?

efe6316

I prefer ....

....

Spot the statue

3 Regarde bien ces trois statues de Paddington. Écoute Martin décrire l'une d'entre elles. Coche celle dont il s'agit.

efe6317

1 ☐ 2 ☐ 3 ☐

Listen to English every day... practice makes perfect!

Guess the password!

4 Écoute et repère où se trouve Paddington. Note ce lieu ci-dessous, ce sera le mot de passe pour le prochain cours d'anglais !

Lieu : ....

efe6318

Pour cette activité, tu auras besoin de la carte de Londres (manuel p. 93).

PROJECT 8 Have fun with art

LESSON 1

"Who are these people?"

Textbook p. 105

Label the painting with:

- elements from Alexa's description ↳ Question 2 b
- elements from Mrs Beth's description ↳ Question 3 b

American Gothic, Grant Wood, 1930

HELP

- an old man
- an old lady
- a farmhouse
- a window
- a pitchfork 
- a rake 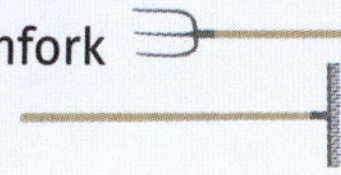
- look plain
- look angry/sad/serious
- look mad at (*somebody*)

LESSON 2

What is she doing?

Textbook p. 106

Time to write Fill in these balloons with the help of Mary's comments.

This is Day in the Life of a Girl. *The story starts up in the left corner, where she is sleeping…*

Here, she is ……………

…………………………………

…………………………………

…………………………………

…………………………………

…………………………………

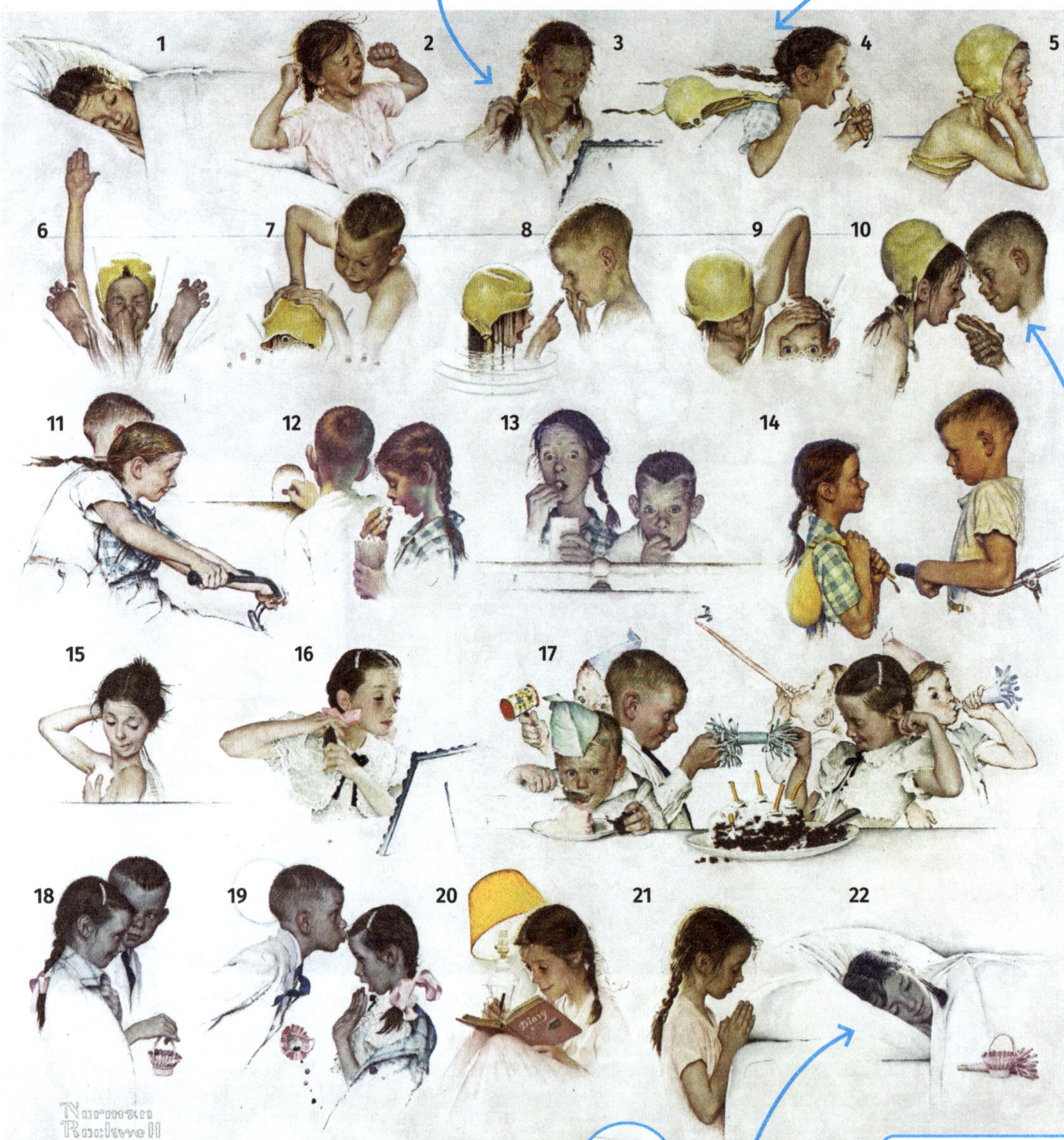

Day in the Life of a Little Girl, Norman Rockwell, 1952

…………………………………

…………………………………

…………………………………

…………………………………

…………………………………

Fais ces exercices sans regarder ton manuel, puis vérifie tes réponses !

Textbook p. 110

AT HOME

Je mémorise

1 ✱ **Écris l'action correspondant à chaque illustration :**

1. ....
....

2. ....
....

3. ....
....

4. ....
....

5. ....
....

2 ✱ **Que font-ils ? Colorie chaque illustration dans la couleur du verbe qui lui correspond.**

stretch | jump | hold hands | push | walk | run

Recopie sous chaque illustration le verbe qui convient.

....

....

....

....

....

....

3 ✱✱ **Complète le cadre avec les informations utiles pour situer des éléments dans une image.**

Fais attention aux prépositions de lieu ! *at*, *on* ou *in* ?

Je m'entraîne

4 **Neuf adjectifs servant à décrire les expressions du visage sont cachés dans cette grille. Combien arriveras-tu à en trouver ?**

J	M	S	V	H	A	P	P	Y	V
S	N	E	R	V	O	U	S	Y	G
U	E	R	Q	T	A	G	Q	D	Z
R	S	I	X	A	N	G	R	Y	D
P	C	O	I	B	L	O	G	A	M
R	A	U	C	O	D	U	M	R	Q
I	R	S	Y	U	U	S	A	D	Y
S	E	M	M	A	D	S	N	S	X
E	D	S	H	O	C	K	E	D	Y
D	M	W	H	I	D	G	N	A	K

Recopie ci-dessous ceux qui caractérisent le plus souvent tes humeurs.

Edward Hopper,
Cape Cod Evening, 1939

5 **Dictation time!** efe6363

Écris les phrases que tu entends.

1. ....
2. ....
3. ....
4. ....

6 **Regarde bien ce tableau.**
Complète sa description en utilisant les mots proposés.

N'oublie pas de conjuguer les verbes !

on the left
on the right
in the middle
in front of

there is
there are

look
stretch

maybe

.... there is a dog.
.... , ... some trees.
...., there is a house,
and .... the house,
.... a man and a woman.
The woman .... bored.
The man .... his arm.
.... he is playing with the dog.

Textbook p. 76

AT HOME

Le Présent *BE* + V-*ing*
(forme affirmative)

1 ✱ **a. Ces phrases décrivent un tableau. Remets les mots dans l'ordre et découvre ce qu'il représente !**

1. man / There / a / is / . / woman / and / a → ....
2. reading / . / The / man / is → ....
3. The / the / . / playing / woman / is / piano → ....
4. dress / . / wearing / She / a / is / red → ....

✱✱ **b. Peux-tu dessiner ce tableau ?** Compare ton dessin avec celui d'un(e) camarade !

2 ✱✱ **Tu assistes à l'enregistrement de l'émission *Kids explain art to experts* et tu envoies des SMS à un(e) ami(e).**
Complète tes commentaires à l'aide des verbes suivants :

have | start | suggest | talk | describe

Conjugue les verbes au Présent *BE* + V-*ing*.

It .... ! I'm so excited!!

Alexa ....
a painting representing a couple. Well, I *think* it's a couple...

The experts ....
together. I think the one on the left has an idea...

Oh, he just buzzed!
He .... an answer!

It's the right answer! Oh my,
I .... so much fun!

3 ✱✱✱ **Encore une nouvelle version de *American Gothic* ! Rédige un petit texte pour la décrire :**

I can see..
....
....
....
....

HELP
• stand • wear • hold
• overalls (*une salopette*)

Le Présent *BE* + V-ing
(formes négative et interrogative)

1 ★ **Les réponses aux questions suivantes ont été mélangées.**
Peux-tu reconstituer les paires ? Ne te mélange pas les pinceaux !

Are Mary and Chuck eating in this vignette? •	• Yes, I am.
Are you drawing a new version of *American Gothic*? •	• No, she isn't.
Why is the boy running? •	• No, they aren't.
Is the lady holding a vase in her hand? •	• I am eating.
What are you doing? •	• Because he is late.

2 ★★ **Explique chaque événement en choisissant un verbe qui convient.**

Attention, dans certains cas il faudra mettre le verbe à la forme négative !

1. The teacher is angry because the pupils ....
2. The cat is scared because ....
3. Great! We can play football today, ...
4. I can't watch TV right now because ....
5. Sorry, I can't hear you because my brother ....

HELP
• play the trumpet • snow • listen • rain • study

3 ★★ **a. Ces phrases sont inexactes par rapport à l'image.**
Réécris-les à la forme négative, puis rétablis la vérité.

1. Raya is wearing a blue T-shirt. → She is not wearing a blue T-shirt. She is wearing a red T-shirt.
2. The dragon is sleeping.
....
....
3. Raya is riding a horse.
....
....
4. Raya is holding a pitchfork.
....
....

* épée = *sword*

★★★ **b. À ton tour, écris deux phrases inexactes par rapport à l'image.**
Prépare-toi à les lire à ton voisin pour qu'il puisse les corriger !
....
....
....

Textbook p. 114

Early finishers

Acting time!

IN GROUPS **Ajoutez d'autres bulles (au moins 5) en déformant les propos des personnages.** ***Have fun!***

Placez les bulles où vous le souhaitez !

- **Vous pouvez vous amuser à changer :**
- Le sujet : Remember Harry... → Remember Mary... → ...
- Le verbe : He is selling his house → He is buying his house → He is eating his house → ...
- Le complément : He is selling his house → He is selling his mouse → He is selling his palace → ...

- **Vous pouvez aussi ajouter :**
- Des adjectifs : He is selling his beautiful house
- Des précisions sur... le lieu : He is selling his house in California.
  la date : He is selling his house on Monday.

The Gossips, Norman Rockwell, 1948

Quiz

1 🔊 e efe6364

Écoute et coche la bonne réponse.

1.	☐ breakfast	☐ lunch	☐ a snack	☐ dinner
2.	☐ at the top	☐ at the bottom	☐ on the left	☐ on the right
3. I am…	☐ getting up	☐ getting dressed	☐ brushing my teeth	☐ getting undressed
4. I am…	☐ getting up	☐ getting dressed	☐ brushing my teeth	☐ getting undressed

Listen up!

Guess the password!

2 🔊 e efe6365

Écoute Mai-Linh expliquer ce qu'elle est en train de faire. Peux-tu deviner de quoi il s'agit ? La réponse sera le mot de passe pour le prochain cours d'anglais !

I know! The answer is:

....

Let's draw!

3 🔊 e efe6366

Écoute cette description d'image. Sauras-tu la dessiner ?

Spot the right description

4 🔊 e efe6367

Regarde bien ce tableau.
Tu vas entendre trois descriptions ; une seule est correcte. Laquelle ?

☐ Description n°1
☐ Description n°2
☐ Description n°3

Edward Hopper,
Room in New York, 1932

PROJECT 9

Junior Rangers

LESSON 1

1. Meet Ranger Ruby

Textbook p. 116

2 b. Complete Ruby's ID card.

JUNIOR RANGER

Name: ....

Age: ....

State: ....

Country: ....

♥ ....

4 Let's recap! What does a Junior Ranger do?

a. Match the beginning and the end of the sentences.

A Junior Ranger...	
completes •	• Junior Ranger badges.
completes •	• national parks.
earns •	• different activities.
explores and protects •	• the Junior Ranger motto.
learns •	• Junior Ranger booklets.

b. Complete this definition:

A Junior Ranger is a young person who ....

....

....

....

2. Take the pledge!

Textbook p. 117

3 Illustrate the pledge with your own drawings.

JUNIOR RANGER PLEDGE

As a Junior Ranger, I want to be a protector of the national parks. When I visit the parks, I pledge[1] that…

1. I will stay on the paths and trails.
2. I will help keep the park clean by not littering[2] or polluting.
3. I will not feed, pet or harass wildlife[3].
4. I will not harm plants, so they will be there for other people to enjoy.
5. I will talk to my friends and family to encourage them to protect the parks, too.

1. 2. 3. *Ruby explains the vocabulary* e efe6402

NEED MORE HELP WITH THE VOCABULARY?
→ *WORDS*, textbook p. 122

1. Three famous parks

Textbook p. 118-119

3 a. Complete your Junior Ranger booklet.

- Write the name of each park and the state it is in.
- Label the pictures.
- Give your impressions!

HELP

- a geyser
- a coral reef
- the Colorado River
- a canyon
- colourful fish
- a hot spring

.... National Park

Location: ....

....

....

My impressions: ....

....

.... National Park

Location: ....

....

....

My impressions: ....

....

.... National Park

Location: ....

....

....

My impressions: ....

....

b. Find where the three parks are on the map and write their names.

For the champions

- Spot Congaree National Park where Ruby was.
- Circle the state where she lives.

Time to write Write a visitor's review about one of these parks.

My Review

.... National Park is ....!

You can see ....

....

....

And you can ....

....

....

I think it is .... and ....!

2. Protect national parks

Textbook p. 119

2 **In groups, explain what you *must* or *must not* do in a national park.**

a. Match the verbs with the right endings.

make •	• a tent
put up •	• on the trail
build •	• noise
stay •	• trees
damage •	• a fire

b. Use these expressions to complete the rules:
→ You must/mustn't…

You ....
....
....

....
....
....

....
....
....

....
....
....

....
....
....

Fais ces exercices sans regarder ton manuel, puis vérifie tes réponses !

Textbook p. 122

AT HOME

Je mémorise

1 ✱ **Légende ce poster avec le plus de mots possible.**
Si tu sais nommer d'autres éléments, tu peux ajouter des flèches !

....

....

....

....

....

....

2 ✱✱ ***Challenge!***
Les noms de 10 animaux sont cachés dans cette grille. Essaie d'en retrouver autant que tu peux et recopie-les ci-dessous.

I	A	B	E	A	V	E	R	A
D	E	E	R	W	H	A	L	E
A	L	L	I	G	A	T	O	R
N	T	Q	E	T	O	Y	O	C
O	L	L	I	D	A	M	R	A
S	N	A	K	E	L	G	A	E
I	P	I	X	E	V	I	E	A
B	S	C	O	R	P	I	O	N
B	U	F	F	A	L	O	W	B

BISON.............................. ....

....

....

....

....

Quel est ton score ? .... / 10

3 **Dictation time!** efe6417

✱✱ **Écris les mots que tu entends.**

1. ....
2. ....
3. ....
4. ....
5. ....
6. ....

4 ✱✱✱ **Peux-tu retrouver les activités définies ci-dessous ?**

1. Taking a long walk, especially for pleasure → ....
2. Spending a holiday living in a tent → ....
3. Chasing and killing wild animals → ....
4. Catching fish → ....

AT HOME

5 **a.** Ce blason représente les parcs nationaux. Peux-tu le légender ?

1. ....

2. ....

3. ....

4. ....

b. Utilise les mots que tu as trouvés pour compléter ce petit texte :

nps.gov

National Parks are special places that protect history, culture and the American story.
If you look at the logo, you will see several elements that are important in National Parks!

- The .... in the distance represents things like scenic beauty, special landforms, and geologic resources.
- The .... represents the different natural resources protected (like trees and plant life).
- The .... represents water resources and the creatures which live in that water.
- The .... represents the wildlife that live inside of national parks.

6 **Crée un logo pour TON parc !**

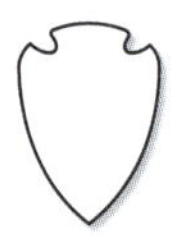

– Quel est son nom ? Qu'est-ce qu'il protège ?
– Dessine le logo, puis explique ce que chaque élément représente.

Inspire-toi du petit texte ci-dessus.

7 **Tu viens d'acheter ces cartes postales sur les parcs nationaux.**
Choisis un parc et explique ce que l'on y voit ou ce que l'on peut y faire. Ton camarade saura-t-il l'identifier ?

....

....

....

....

....

....

....

....

....

....

....

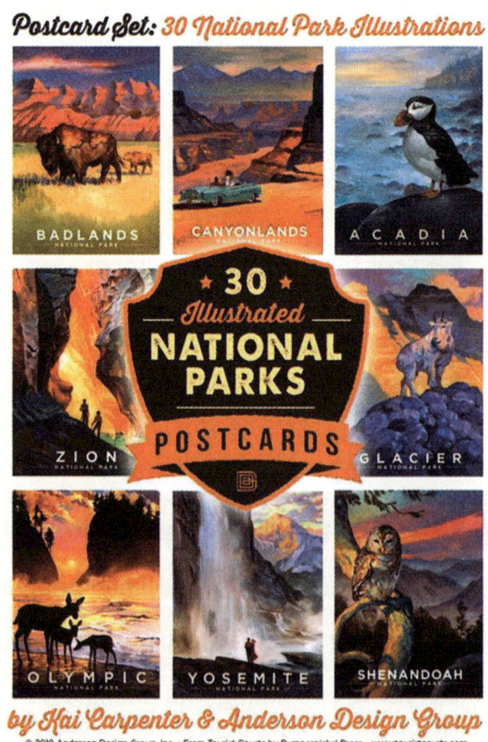

WILL

AT HOME

1 ★ Prépare-toi à devenir Junior Ranger ! Complète cet engagement avec *will* ou *won't*.

JUNIOR RANGER PLEDGE

As a Junior Ranger, I promise I........................... protect the plants, animals and water.

I .... scare animals because that is dangerous.

I .... preserve the history of our National Parks.

I .... continue to explore and protect our resources.

I .... put myself at risk.

I .... share what I know with others.

2 ★★ **a.** Coche les promesses que devra faire ce futur Junior Ranger lorsqu'il prêtera serment :

- ☐ I will explore the park
- ☐ I will pick flowers.
- ☐ I won't be quiet.
- ☐ I will litter.
- ☐ I won't scare the animals.

b. Corrige les phrases qui sont fausses :

....

....

3 ★★ Le Junior Ranger est maintenant prêt à répondre aux questions du Ranger.
Note les réponses attendues à droite.

1. Will you preserve nature?
2. Will you explore the national parks?
3. Will you feed animals?
4. Will you teach others what you know?
5. Will you scare animals?

1. I will preserve nature.
2. ....
3. ....
4. ....
5. ....

4 ★★★ Te voilà Ranger ! Prépare ton discours de bienvenue à un groupe de Junior Rangers.

Welcome to Grand Canyon National Park!
We have some great activities for you this weekend! Tomorrow we will...

HELP
- go hiking
- ride a bike through the park
- ...

MUST

1 ★ **Entraîne-toi pour devenir Junior Ranger ! Associe chaque panneau à sa consigne.**

You can pick apples. | You mustn't hunt. | You can pick flowers. | You mustn't make noise.

2 ★★ **Tu visites le parc de Yosemite avec ta famille, quelle chance !**
Explique à ton petit frère ce qu'il a le droit de faire ou pas.

Complète les phrases à l'aide de *must* – *can* – *mustn't* en t'aidant des panneaux.

1. You .... be quiet ! → n°........
2. You .... ride your bike here. → n°........
3. You .... park here! → n°........
4. Pedestrians .... use this trail. → n°........
5. It's OK – we .... walk the dog here! → n°........
6. Be careful, you .... feed animals,
   it's not good for them! → n°........

3 ★★★ **Peux-tu rédiger le règlement de ce parc ?**
Utilise les instructions des panneaux.

1. ....
2. ....
3. ....
4. ....
5. ....

Listen up!

Challenge

🔊 e efe6418

1 Écoute et entoure un maximum d'animaux nommés par Ruby. Combien en as-tu reconnu ?

BUG BISON BIRDS EAGLE

ELK COYOTE DEER

BEAVER BEAR

FISH

Note celui que tu adorerais voir :

………………………………………………… .

Celui qui t'effraie le plus :

………………………………………………… .

Beware of bears!

🔊 e efe6419

2 Écoute Ruby t'expliquer comment réagir face à un ours ! Dessine des panneaux pour illustrer deux de ces règles.

Guessing game

🔊 e efe6420

3 Écoute et coche la carte postale qui correspond au parc évoqué.

Guess the password

🔊 e efe6421

4 Ruby te fait deviner un parc national. Écoute-la et identifie le parc. Son nom sera le mot de passe pour le prochain cours d'anglais !

I know! The answer is: …………………………………………

PROJECT 10 Coming to America

LESSON 1

Welcome to the American Immigration Museum!

Textbook p. 128-129

2 The museum gave you this Visitor's Activity Guide.
Make links between the short texts and the pictures.

Time to write Use the audio guide to add extra information. efe6450

Start the TOUR!

Irish Farmers, 1888
Ireland = in Europe

>1 Many people emigrated to America from Europe in the 19th and 20th centuries. They migrated for various reasons.

Extra information:

....

....

....

....

>2 Immigrants travelled by boat. The ships sometimes carried 3,000 people at one time.

Extra information:

....

....

....

....

....

Immigration ship, 1906

New York Harbor, 1952

>3 For many immigrants, the first view of America was the Statue of Liberty.

Extra information:

....

....

....

....

>4 At Ellis Island, officers asked immigrants many questions.

Extra information:

....

....

....

....

....

....

Interview at Ellis Island, 1950

Manhattan, New York, 1930s

>5 After leaving Ellis Island, immigrants started a new life in America.

Extra information:

....

....

....

....

....

Check your answers with the class.

MINI TASK

Record an audio guide.

The museum needs an audio guide for these three pictures.

1. Look at the new pictures and captions. What can you say about them?
2. Choose one picture. Write two or three sentences to describe it.
3. Practise reading your script aloud, then record yourself.

Immigrants arriving in America, 1923

Arriving at Ellis Island, 1926

Looking at Manhattan with hope, 1925

LESSON 2

Meet Gabriella!

Textbook p. 130

3 **Need help?** Here is a guided version of the text:

Regarde bien les verbes. Gabriella parle-t-elle du passé ou du présent ?

Regarde les indications de temps. Elles t'aideront à comprendre le déroulement de l'histoire de Gabriella.

Entoure les adjectifs en rouge. Ils te permettront de comprendre les sentiments et les premières impressions de Gabriella.

Three months ago, I moved to Austin, Texas, to learn English. I didn't know any English when I got here. My mother, sister, brother, aunt, grandmother, and I drove from our ranch in Coahuila, Mexico, to our new apartment in Austin. [...]

I was worried and excited to move. I didn't know people here; I didn't know things. I was really scared at first. My hardest moment was when I started school. At first, homework was really hard because everything was in English... [...]

I like a lot about America. I especially like my teachers. They are really nice here and very helpful. I like the stores and the mall. My favorite music is hip-hop and rock. I love to read books that are scary, funny, and beautiful. My favorite American foods are macaroni and hamburgers.

Time to write

Complete Gabriella's information card.

NAME: Gabriella AGE: 13 GRADE: 7th

CURRENT HOME:

DETAILS ABOUT HER LIFE BEFORE:

DETAILS ABOUT HER LIFE NOW:

EMOTIONS AND FEELINGS:

MINI TASK! Textbook p. 131

Discover another young American. (IN PAIRS)

1. Choose a text and complete the child's information card.
2. Share his story with your partner. Are there any similarities between the two stories?

NAME: Vandi AGE: 12 GRADE: 6th

CURRENT HOME:

DETAILS ABOUT HIS LIFE BEFORE:

DETAILS ABOUT HIS LIFE NOW:

EMOTIONS AND FEELINGS:

NAME: Taylor AGE: 11 GRADE: 4th

CURRENT HOME:

DETAILS ABOUT HIS LIFE BEFORE:

DETAILS ABOUT HIS LIFE NOW:

EMOTIONS AND FEELINGS:

WORDS

Fais ces exercices sans regarder ton manuel, puis vérifie tes réponses !

Textbook p. 134

AT HOME

Je mémorise

1 ★ **Propose des adjectifs pour qualifier des émotions positives et des émotions négatives.**

....	....
....	....
....	....

2 ★ **En image !**
Relie chaque dessin à l'adjectif qu'il illustre.

difficult | tired | helpful | amazing

3 ★★ **Complète ces témoignages de nouveaux venus aux États-Unis : ajoute des adverbes permettant de préciser leur pensée.**

really | too | a little | especially

1. I was excited to come to the USA, and I was only .... scared about learning English.
2. I wanted to try every food in America, ... turkey on Thanksgiving.
3. When the teachers talked .... fast, I didn't understand anything.
4. All in all, coming to America was a .... good experience.

4 ★★ **Voici quatre expériences d'immigration aux États-Unis. Pour chacune, imagine le moyen de transport probablement utilisé.**

1. A boy moved from Mexico to Texas in 2019. → ....
2. A family came to the USA from Europe in 2017. → ....
3. A man travelled to the US from England in 1911. → ....
4. Immigrants in New York moved to California this year. → ....

5 ★★★ **Écoute quelqu'un parler de ses premiers jours aux États-Unis.** e efe6460

a. Coche la série de photos qui correspond à son expérience.

1. ☐

2. ☐

3. ☐

b. Choisis une autre série, et écris le témoignage correspondant.

....
....
....
....
....
....
....

AT HOME

6 ✱ **Ton top 3 ! Quelles activités ou traditions américaines aimerais-tu le plus essayer ?**

....

....

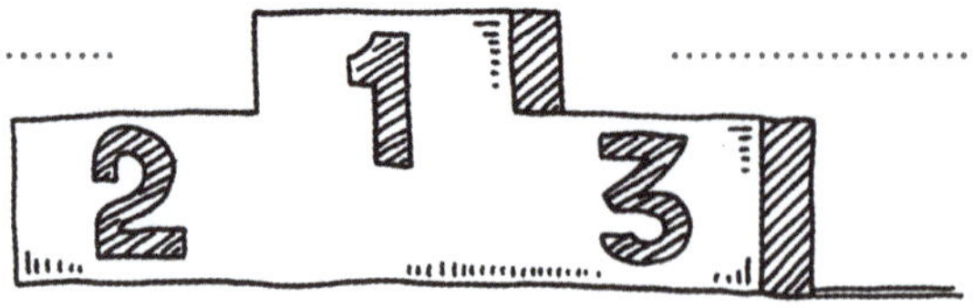

7 ✱✱ **Tu as trouvé une veille carte postale des années 1900, mais certains mots ont été effacés. Imagine ce qui a pu être écrit.**

Dear Carmine,

It was very .... to leave Italy. I wanted to stay with my friends and the rest of my family. On the boat, I was .... about not speaking English. Then I saw it – the Statue of Liberty. Immediately I felt .... about the great possibilities in my future.

Write to me soon,

Michael

8 ✱✱ **D'après toi, chacune de ces phrases est-elle vraie ou fausse ? Coche ta réponse.**

1. In the early 1900s, most immigrants arrived by plane. ☐ Vrai ☐ Faux
2. Immigrants are always happy to leave their home country. ☐ Vrai ☐ Faux
3. Some immigrants have good experiences in the USA. ☐ Vrai ☐ Faux
4. Immigrants to the USA only come from one or two other countries. ☐ Vrai ☐ Faux

9 ✱✱✱ **Écoute ce témoignage et complète le tableau avec les mots que tu reconnais.** efe6461

feelings/descriptions	immigrating	adapting
....	....	....
....	....	....
....	....	....
....	....	....

Le Prétérit simple

1 ★ **Complète ces phrases en mettant les verbes au Prétérit.**

1. In the early 1900s, many immigrants .... by boat. (*arrive*)
2. Some people .... because of famine. (*emigrate*)
3. New immigrants .... new traditions. (*discover*)
4. Children of immigrants .... school immediately. (*start*)

2 ★★ **Choisis le verbe qui convient pour compléter chaque phrase. Conjugue-le au Prétérit.**

move | search | enter | decide

1. In the early 1900s, many people .... to emigrate to the United States.
2. More than 70% of immigrants .... the U.S. through New York City.
3. New immigrants .... for jobs in New York.
4. After some years, some families .... to different parts of the country.

3 ★★ **Complète ces phrases en conjuguant le verbe *BE* à la forme qui convient :**

1. At the end of the 19th century, most immigrants .... from Germany, Ireland and England.
2. Life .... not easy for new immigrants.
3. It .... sometimes difficult to find a job and the salaries .... low.

4 ★★ **Un nouvel élève vient d'arriver dans ta classe aux États-Unis, en provenance d'un pays étranger. Pose-lui une question, puis imagine sa réponse !**

How did you learn English?

I learned it at school.

How When Where	travel live before arrive learn English

....

....

....

5 **Écoute Mark te parler de son grand-père.** e efe6462

★★ **a. Coche les images selon qu'elles correspondent (✓) ou pas (✗) à son expérience.**

 ☐  ☐  ☐  ☐  ☐  ☐

★★★ **b. Peux-tu résumer cette expérience en quelques lignes ?**

....

....

....

Focus sur les verbes irréguliers

1 ★ **Complète ces échanges en mettant les verbes au Prétérit :**

1. When did you leave home? → I .... home four days ago.
2. Did you drive here? → Yes, I .... all the way from Mexico City.
3. How long did it take you? → It .... me four days.
4. Did you come on your own? → No, I .... with my family.

Consulte la liste des verbes irréguliers dans ton manuel p. 158

2 ★★ **À toi maintenant de poser les questions ! Fais bien attention au choix de l'auxiliaire.**

1. How did you .... here?
   I came here by plane.
2. How .... ?
   I felt very excited!
3. How .... your trip?
   Our trip was fine, and not too long.
4. Did .... an apartment easily?
   Yes, very easily! We found an apartment on the day we arrived!

3 ★★ **Reconstitue quatre phrases à propos des jeunes immigrés rencontrés p. 130-131 du manuel.**

1. Gabriella and her family .... (*drive*) •
2. Taylor .... (*feel*) •
3. Vandi's mom .... (*make*) •
4. Many immigrants .... (*eat*) •

- • different foods in their home countries.
- • turkey on Thanksgiving this year.
- • from Mexico to Texas.
- • a little nervous about moving.

4 ★★★ **Tu viens d'arriver aux États-Unis. Utilise les mots ci-dessous pour écrire une page de ton journal.**

come | drive | feel | make | eat | see

Today, we drove from Mexico to Texas. ....

....

....

....

....

....

....

....

....

Spot the picture

1 Regarde bien ces deux îles. Écoute David parler de l'une d'elles et coche la bonne image.

efe6463

☐ Ellis Island

☐ Liberty Island

Story time

efe6464

2 Ces images illustrent le témoignage que tu vas entendre, mais elles sont toutes mélangées ! Écoute et numérote-les dans le bon ordre.

Listen up!

Guess the password!

efe6465

3 Écris les mots que tu entends en plaçant une lettre sur chaque pointillé. Si tu les as bien orthographiés, tu devrais trouver le mot mystère ! Ce sera le mot de passe pour ton prochain cours d'anglais !

… … … …   … … …

… … … … … … …

… … … … … … … … …

… … … …

Le mot mystère est : … … … … …

Fiches & activités

Mémo Grammaire — BE au Présent

Textbook p. 17

À quoi ça sert ?

Le verbe *BE* est très utile pour se présenter ! Tu peux l'utiliser pour dire :

- qui tu es — I .... Grace.
- quel âge tu as — I .... 11.
- d'où tu es, où tu habites — I .... from Connecticut.

Hi! I .... Grace.
Nice to meet you!

À l'oral, il est fréquent de 'contracter' le verbe *BE*.

Comment ça marche ?

	Conjugaison de *BE*
1re personne du singulier	I .... Grace. I .... American.
3e personne du singulier	What .... your name? My name .... Grace.

À l'oral on peut dire :

I .... American.

What .... your name?

Mémo Grammaire — Les pronoms personnels

Textbook p. 21

À quoi ça sert ?

Les pronoms personnels permettent de désigner des personnes ou des choses, comme en français.

Comment ça marche ?

.... say "yes"!

- Pour parler de moi, j'utilise ....
- Pour désigner la ou les personnes à qui je m'adresse, j'utilise ....

Are .... from London?

- Pour désigner un ensemble d'autres personnes, j'utilise ....

The Beatles are British. .... are from Liverpool.

Récapitule les pronoms que tu connais :

je	....
tu / vous	....
ils / elles	....

I prend toujours une majuscule.

Mémo Grammaire — There is... / There are...

Textbook p. 25

From *The Wimpy Kid Do-It-Yourself Book*, by Jeff Kinney

À quoi ça sert ?

Pour indiquer la présence de quelqu'un ou de quelque chose,

on peut utiliser .... ou ....

In Greg's brain, ... music and movies.

Comment ça marche ?

- On utilise *there* suivi du verbe ...., qui s'accorde avec le .... mot qui suit.

There	....	+ 1er mot <u>au singulier</u>	In Greg's brain, ... <u>food</u> and sleep.
	....	+ 1er mot <u>au pluriel</u>	In Greg's brain, ... <u>video games</u> and TV.

- Pour interroger : What .... in Greg's brain?

Mémo Grammaire — L'article *a (an)*

Textbook p. 29

À quoi ça sert ?

Il s'emploie un peu comme l'article indéfini *un/une* en français.

In my schoolbag, there is .... ruler, ... glue stick, . . .

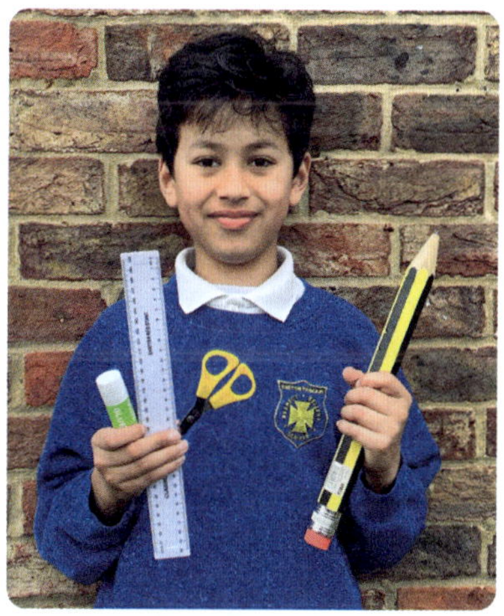

Comment ça marche ?

- L'article *a* devient .... devant un <u>son voyelle</u>, pour faire la liaison.

  In my pencil case, there is .... eraser.

- Devant des noms indéfinis au ...., on emploie « l'article zéro ».

  In my bag, there are Ø textbooks.

- On peut utiliser *a* et *an* avec des noms masculins ou féminins.

  In my class, there is .... English boy and .... Scottish girl.

Mémo Grammaire — L'impératif

Textbook p. 40

À quoi ça sert ?

On utilise l'impératif pour donner un ....

ou un ....

.... a pumpkin pie!

Comment ça marche ?

- À la forme **affirmative**, on utilise simplement la ....

.... a costume.

- À la forme **négative**, la base verbale est précédée de .... *(qui est la contraction de ....)*

.... forget to brush your teeth!

Mémo Grammaire — *HAVE* au Présent simple

Textbook p. 41

À quoi ça sert ?

On peut utiliser le verbe *HAVE* pour dire ce que l'on ....

I .... a zombie costume.

She .... a witch costume.

We .... lots of candy!

Comment ça marche ?

On utilise .... à toutes les personnes,

sauf à la 3e personne du singulier où on utilise ....

Who .... chocolate kisses?

Conjugaison de *HAVE*

I ....

You ....

He / she / it ....

We ....

You ....

They ....

Mémo Grammaire – Les déterminants possessifs

Textbook p. 52

À quoi ça sert ?

On utilise les déterminants possessifs pour indiquer à qui appartient un objet ou pour exprimer un lien entre des personnes.

Complète cette liste !

my
....
his / her
its*
....
....
....

* pour un objet ou un animal non familier

Comment ça marche ?

En anglais, le déterminant possessif s'accorde avec ....
en genre et **en nombre**

...his... glasses

.... glasses

Tom and Derek play music.
.... band is called 'Dog Zombies'.

Mémo Grammaire – Le génitif

Textbook p. 53

À quoi ça sert ?

Le 's indique un lien de parenté **ou de** possession **entre deux éléments.**

Parenté : We're Tom's parents.

Possession : This is Derek's dog.

Comment ça marche ?

- On utilise la marque du génitif ...., en faisant bien attention à l'ordre des mots !

le professeur de Tom
....

- Et si le nom du possesseur se termine **déjà** par un -s ?

→ Si ce -s est la marque du **pluriel**, alors **on ajoute uniquement** .... :

Uncle Kevin is my cousins' father.

→ Si ce -s n'est pas la marque du pluriel, **alors on ajoute** .... :

Tom is in Marcus's class.

Mémo Grammaire — Le Présent simple (forme affirmative)

Textbook p. 64

À quoi ça sert ?

On utilise le Présent simple pour donner des informations (par exemple sur des traditions culturelles ou familiales).

They .... the tree together.

Comment ça marche ?

- On utilise la .... à toutes les personnes, sauf à la 3e personne du singulier où on ajoute un « .... » à la base verbale.

The Queen .... Christmas at Sandringham Castle.

- Rappel : *BE* et *HAVE* au Présent simple

BE	
I	We ....
You	You ....
He / she / it	They ....

HAVE	
I	We ....
You	You ....
He / she / it	They ....

Mémo Grammaire — Le Présent simple (formes négative et interrogative)

Textbook p. 65

Comment ça marche ?

- On a besoin d'un .... pour former les questions : et les négations :

.... they <u>spend</u> Christmas in London?

In France, we .... <u>pull</u> Christmas crackers.

- <u>Le verbe</u> est toujours à la ....
C'est l'auxiliaire qui porte la marque de la conjugaison :

.... the Queen <u>spend</u> Christmas at Buckingham Palace?

À la 3e personne du singulier, *DO* devient ....

- Si le verbe est .... on n'a pas besoin d'un autre auxiliaire car .... se suffit à lui-même.

.... you excited about the holidays?

Forme interrogative

Traditions .... the same in England and in France.

Forme négative

Mémo
Grammaire Les adjectifs qualificatifs

Textbook p. 76

À quoi ça sert ?

- On utilise les adjectifs qualificatifs pour apporter des précisions à propos d'un ....

Real witches dress in ordinary clothes.

- On place les adjectifs dans un ordre bien précis : taille, forme, couleur, qualité.

a big blue hat.

Comment ça marche ?

- En anglais, les adjectifs sont .... :

1. This witch has a black hat.
2. Witches wear black hats.

- En (1), le nom *cat* est au ....
- En (2), le nom *cat* est au ....
- La forme de l'adjectif
  ☐ change ☐ reste inchangée

- Lorsqu'ils sont **épithètes**, on place les adjectifs .... le **nom** qu'ils qualifient.

Real witches live in ordinary houses.

Souligne les noms et entoure les adjectifs dans cet exemple.

Mémo
Grammaire Les questions (2)

Textbook p. 77

Comment ça marche ?

- Pour poser des questions en anglais, on a besoin d'un auxiliaire, par exemple *DO* ou *BE*.

.... witches dangerous?

.... witches like children?

- Il existe deux grands types de questions :
  → Les questions fermées : ce sont celles auxquelles on répond par ....

.... witches like children?

.... witches nasty?

Ordre des mots dans ces questions :

DO + ... + verbe + ?

BE + ... + adjectif + ?

BE est à la fois auxiliaire et verbe, il se suffit à lui-même !

→ Les questions ouvertes : elles commencent par un mot .... que l'on choisit en fonction du type d'information qu'on veut obtenir.

How .... you recognize witches?

Where .... they live?

Ordre des mots dans ces questions :

Mot interrogatif + auxiliaire + ... (+ V + ?)

Mémo Grammaire — Le nom en V + *-ing* (1)

Textbook p. 88

À quoi ça sert ?

- **L'ajout de la terminaison *-ing* à une base verbale permet de fabriquer un ....**

> My hobbies are jujitsu, fight......... and sing......... !

- On peut ensuite s'en servir pour dire ce qu'on aime faire (ou pas !) en utilisant des verbes comme *like, love, enjoy, hate*...

> I .... going to the arcade.

Comment ça marche ?

- **Il suffit d'ajouter *-ing* à la .... :** surf → surf.........
- **Sauf que... ce n'est pas si simple ! Il faut faire attention à l'orthographe.**
  - → Quand le verbe se termine par un « e », on .... ce « e » :

    dance → .... skate → ....

  - → Quand le verbe comporte .... syllabe et se termine par « consonne-voyelle-consonne », on .... la dernière consonne :

    swim → .... run → ....

Mémo Grammaire — Les adverbes de fréquence

Textbook p. 89

À quoi ça sert ?

On les utilise pour préciser à quelle .... (souvent, parfois, rarement, jamais...) on fait quelque chose.
→ Par exemple, Kai se réveille habituellement à 6h30. Il dirait donc :

> I .... wake up at 6.30 am.

Comment ça marche ?

- **On choisit l'adverbe de fréquence qui correspond à ce que l'on veut dire :**

always – sometimes – never – often – usually

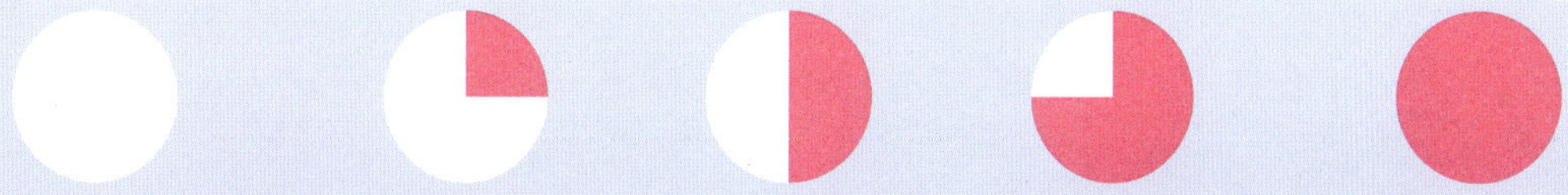

....

- **On le place au bon endroit dans la phrase.**
  - → Après le verbe *BE* :

    I am .... at the beach at 6.30 am.

  - → Avant tous les autres verbes :

    We .... play together.

Mémo Grammaire CAN

Textbook p. 100

À quoi ça sert ?

Pour parler de ce qui est :

✔ possible, autorisé, ou de ce que l'on est capable de faire, on utilise : C............

She .... cook quite well!

✘ impossible, interdit, ou de ce que l'on ne sait pas faire, on utilise :

C............ ou sa forme contractée C............

You .... eat or drink here.

Comment ça marche ?

- *CAN* est un auxiliaire :
  → Il accompagne un verbe qui est toujours à la ....
  → Il sert à construire les .... et les ....

What .... you do there?

If you .... get tickets, try another theatre.

- *CAN* ne change pas de forme, quel que soit le sujet.

I .... speak English and my penpal .... speak French. It's perfect!

Mémo Grammaire Le nom en V + *-ing* (2)

Textbook p. 100

À quoi ça sert ?

[Rappel] En anglais, on peut fabriquer un .... en ajoutant la terminaison *-ing* à une base verbale. On peut en fabriquer à volonté !

visit London → How about ....?

sit in Hyde Park → I enjoy ....

suggest places to visit → Thanks for ....

Comment ça marche ?

- Il suffit généralement d'ajouter la terminaison *-ing* à la base verbale.
- Mais rappelle-toi, il faut faire attention à l'orthographe !
  → Quand le verbe se termine par un « ...... », on .... ce « ...... » :

share → ....

change → ....

→ Quand le verbe comporte ...... syllabe et se termine par « consonne-voyelle-consonne », on .... la dernière consonne :

shop → ....

Mémo Grammaire — Le Présent en Be + V-ing (forme affirmative)

Textbook p. 112

À quoi ça sert ?

Alors que le Présent simple permet de donner une simple information,

The museum opens at 10 a.m.

le Présent *BE* + V-*ing* permet de faire « plus que cela » :
par exemple expliquer ou commenter.

The man .... hold...... his pitchfork.

The woman .... look...... to the right.

Comment ça marche ?

On utilise l'auxiliaire .... que l'on conjugue au **Présent**.

\+

On ajoute la terminaison .... à la base verbale.

The woman .... look...... to the right.
BV

Conjugaison de *LOOK*

I ....
You ....
He/she/it ....
We ....
You ....
They ....

- Attention à l'orthographe !

describe → She is ....
sit → ....

Mémo Grammaire — Le Présent en *Be* + V-*ing* (formes interrogative et négative)

Textbook p. 113

Comment ça marche ?

- On se sert de l'auxiliaire .... pour construire les phrases interrogatives et négatives :

BE passe devant le .... dans les **questions** : .... she reading?

Il porte la marque de la **négation**. No, she .... reading.

- *BE* est repris dans les réponses brèves :

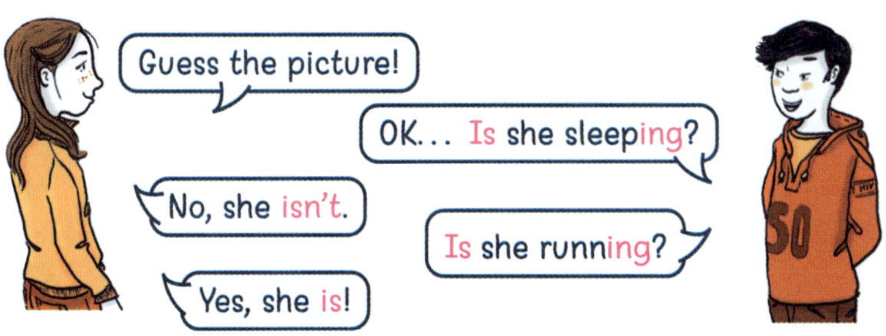

Mémo Grammaire WILL

Textbook p. 124

À quoi ça sert ?

On utilise *WILL* pour se projeter dans .... et parler de ce qui a de fortes chances de se réaliser (parce que le contexte ou les circonstances s'y prêtent, ou parce qu'on en a l'intention).

I .... stay on the paths and trails.

Comment ça marche ?

- Comme *CAN* (vu au chapitre 7), *WILL* :
  → accompagne un verbe qui est toujours à la ....
  → sert à construire les .... et les ....

.... you visit Death Valley?

No, I ....

→ ne change pas de forme, quel que soit le sujet.

I .... cut wood and she .... make a campfire.

- À l'oral, *WILL* est généralement contracté.

I .... stay on the paths.

I .... feed the animals.

Mémo Grammaire MUST

Textbook p. 125

À quoi ça sert ?

On utilise l'auxiliaire de modalité *MUST* pour exprimer :

- une obligation — You .... respect the animals.
- une interdiction — You .... make noise.

Comment ça marche ?

- Comme *CAN* et comme *WILL*, *MUST* :
  → ne change pas de forme, quel que soit le sujet.
  → accompagne un verbe qui est toujours à la ....
  → sert à construire les .... et les ....

In national parks, you .... always pick up your trash and you .... light fires.

.... you take the Junior Ranger pledge?

- À l'oral, *MUST NOT* est généralement contracté.

You .... pick flowers.

Mémo Grammaire — Le Prétérit simple

Textbook p. 136

À quoi ça sert ?

On utilise le Prétérit simple pour parler d'événements ....

In the 19th and 20th centuries, many people emigrated to America.

Comment ça marche ?

- Pour former le Prétérit simple des verbes réguliers, on ajoute à la base verbale la terminaison .... à toutes les personnes.

The trip across the Atlantic **last**......... two weeks.

- Pour construire les questions, les négations et les réponses courtes, on utilise l'auxiliaire *DO* au Prétérit : ....

.... you travel with your family?

Yes, I .... / No, I .... with my family.

- Le cas de *BE*

BE est un verbe irrégulier. Il a deux formes au Prétérit :

The journey .... hard.

.... you very tired?

Conjugaison de *BE* :

I, he, she, it	....	in America.
we, you, they	....	in America.

Mémo Grammaire — Focus sur les verbes irréguliers

Textbook p. 137

Certains verbes, comme *BE* et *DO* que tu connais déjà, ont un Prétérit irrégulier.

I .... very excited when I .... here.
(get)

Comment ça marche ?

- Il faut les apprendre par cœur ! Tu en trouveras une liste dans ton manuel p. 158.

We .... from our ranch in Coahuila, Mexico.
(drive)

- Comme pour les verbes réguliers, on construit les questions et les négations avec l'auxiliaire *DO* au Prétérit (..........).

When .... you get here?

Level 1 • Easy

I have the **first card.**

Who has a **bat**?

I have a **bat.**

Who has a **spider web**?

I have a **pumpkin.**

Who has a **witch**?

I have a **witch.**

Who has a **ghost**?

I have a **black cat.**

Who has **sweets**?

I have **sweets.**

Who has a **skeleton**?

Level 1 • Easy

I have
a **spider web**.

Who has a **pumpkin**?

I have a **skeleton**.

Who has a **devil**?

I have a **ghost**.

Who has a **black cat**?

I have a **monster**.

Who has a **mummy**?

I have a **devil**.

Who has a **monster**?

I have
a **mummy**.

I have
the **last card**.

Level 2 • Intermediate

START

who has

I have

who has

I have

who has

I have

who has

I have

who has

I have

who has

Level 2 • Intermediate

I have

who has

I have

who has

I have

who has

I have

who has

I have

who has

I have

FINISH

Pour créer ton marque-page, plie suivant cette ligne et colle les deux faces.

MINI TASK !

Textbook p. 93

Instructions

underline

match

circle

cross

tick

highlight

Actions

listen

speak

ask / answer

read

write

look

mime

take

open ≠ close

spell

play

sit down

raise your hand

MINI TASK !

Textbook p. 105

Draw your own version of the painting *American Gothic*.

Artist*: .... **Date:** ....

Title: ....

* write your name!

Drama club

Textbook p. 144

....

....

....

....

....

....

1 b. Write the poem under the corresponding pictures.
Then make links between the pictures and the words in the poem.

c. Swap workbooks with a classmate and check each other's work.

Références des images

1 (bg) ©Laura Ashman/Text and illustration © Liz Pichon, 2014 The right of Liz Pichon to be identified as the author of this work has been asserted by her. ; **1 (bd)** ti-ja/E+/Gettyimages ; **1 (hm)** mariva16/Istock ; **3 (9)** WENN Rights Ltd/Alamy ; **4, 3 (hd, 1)** Paul Wood/US Department of Education ; **7 (mg)** Ben Molyneux/Alamy ; **7 (bg)** "Harry Potter and the sorcerer's stone", 2001. Réal. Chris Columbus. Daniel Radcliffe, Emma Watson, Ruppert Grint. Collection Christophel © Warner Bros. / Heyday Films ; **7 (mbm)** with Michael Gambon, Collection Christophel © Warner Bros./Heyday Films ; **7 (md)** Collection Christophel © Warner Bros./Heyday Films ; **8 (4m)** Silvio-stock.adobe.com ; **8 (4g)** Neftali/Alamy ; **8 (3)** Ridofranz/GettyImages ; **8 (4d)** Ivan Vdovin/Alamy ; **9 (2)** Maryco-stock.adobe.com ; **10 (m)** carterart/Vecteezy ; **10 (b)** Kevenodes/Vecteezy ; **11 (hd)** Black Country Images/Alamy ; **13 (mg)** naumoid/IStock ; **13 (md)** Ian Gavan/GettyImages Europe/GettyImages via AFP ; **14** Dessins librement inspirés de *The Wimpy Kid* by Jeff Kinney pour illustrer les propos des élèves ; **16, 17 (mg1, bd)** New Africa-stock.adobe.com ; **16 (b)** Syda Productions-stock.adobe.com ; **16 (hg2, hd2)** Pixel-Shot-stock.adobe.com ; **16 (hg3)** splitov27-stock.adobe.com ; **16 (hg1)** snvv-stock.adobe.com ; **16, 17 (hd3, md3, mm)** vorens-stock.adobe.com ; **16 (mg3)** chat_a4-stock.adobe.com ; **16 (mg2)** nata8_vkusidey-stock.adobe.com ; **16 (md2)** Ruberball/Alamy ; **16 (md1)** takoburito/iStockphoto ; **17 (mg)** McIninch/iStockphoto ; **17 (bm)** kcline/iStockphoto ; **17 (md)** malerapaso/iStockphoto ; **18 (hm)** pamela_d_mcadams-stock.adobe.com ; **18 (hd)** boxerx-stock.adobe.com ; **18, 19 (mhm, mhg)** pixelrobot-stock.adobe.com ; **18 (mhd)** picsfive-stock.adobe.com ; **18 (mg)** hudiemm/iStockphoto ; **18 (mm)** angelo19-stock.adobe.com ; **18 (md)** vladvm50-stock.adobe.com ; **18 (mbg)** Christian Bernd-stock.adobe.com ; **18 (mbm)** V.R. Murralinath-stock.adobe.com ; **18 (mbd)** L. Bouvier-stock.adobe.com ; **18 (bg)** Pixel-Shot-stock.adobe.com ; **18 (bm)** subjug/iStockphoto ; **18 (bd)** Kasoga-stock.adobe.com ; **19 (hm)** alexshyripa/AdobeStock ; **19 (hd)** Tarzhanova/AdobeStock ; **19 (mhd)** picsfive/123rf ; **19 (mm)** Africa Studio/AdobeStock ; **19 (md)** gonzalocalle/AdobeStock ; **19 (bg)** Natalia Samorod/AdobeStock ; **19 (bd)** Primastock/AdobeStock ; **23 (hd)** valentinrussanov/GettyImages ; **24 (h1)** Jose Luis Pelaez Inc. / GettyImages ; **24 (b2)** Westend61/GettyImages ; **24 (b3)** Paul Bradbury/Agefotostock ; **24 (b4)** Creativel/iStockphoto ; **24 (h2)** Innovated Captures - stock.adobe.com ; **24 (h3)** McIninch/iStockphoto ; **24 (h4)** Faiz - stock.adobe.com ; **24, 28 (m1, md)** C Squared Studios/GettyImages ; **24 (m2)** Yongyut Khasawng-123RF ; **24 (m3)** McIninch/iStockphoto ; **24 (b1)** Syda Production/Agefotostock ; **24 (m4)** Lynne Mitchell/iStockphoto ; **26 (hg)** karenfoleyphotography/Alamy ; **26 (hd)** hanneliese/AdobeStock ; **26 (mhg)** David Pimborough/AdobeStock ; **26 (mhd)** memoriesarecaptures/iStockphoto ; **26 (mg)** Raymond C. Eichelberger/Shutterstock ; **26 (md)** evemilla/iStockphoto ; **26 (mbg)** Isabelle Cassini/Alamy ; **26 (mbd)** Hayati Kayhan/AdobeStock ; **26 (bg)** zgurski1980/AdobeStock ; **26 (bd)** Jiri Hera/AdobeStock ; **27 (hd)** paci77/GettyImages ; **28 (hg)** Eric D ricochet69 / Alamy ; **29, 3 (h, 2)** Designed by kjpargeter/Freepik ; **30, 101 (md, bg, bm)** Picture Partners / Alamy ; **32, 34 (b, hg, hd, mg)** Text and illustration © Liz Pichon, 2011 The right of Liz Pichon to be identified as the author of this work has been asserted by her ; **32, 33 (hd, h)** Text and illustration © Liz Pichon, 2021 The right of Liz Pichon to be identified as the author of this work has been asserted by her ; **32, 3 (hm, mm, 3)** Text and illustration © Liz Pichon, 2014, 2019 The right of Liz Pichon to be identified as the author of this work has been asserted by her ; **34 (bd)** Texte and illustrations © Liz Pichon, 2020 The right of Liz Pichon to be identified as the author of this work has been asserted by her ; **37 (bm)** Yuri Arcus/Fotolia ; **37 (bg)** Mat Hayward-stock.adobe.com ; **37 (bd)** Beboy/Fotolia ; **37 (hm)** Yacobchuk Olena - stock.adobe.com ; **37 (md)** Eleonore H - stock.adobe.com ; **37 (hd)** Dobrila Vignjevic/Istock ; **37 (mm)** laflor/iStockphoto ; **37 (mg)** shapecharge/iStockphoto ; **39** with Daniel Radcliffe, Warner Bros/Heyday Films © Collection Christophel ; **41, 42 (D, md)** inarik-stock.adobe.com ; **41, 42 (C, mm)** Andrew Paterson/Alamy Stock Photo ; **41, 42 (B, hd)** AnnaPustynnikova/iStockphoto ; **41, 42 (A, hg)** WPA Pool/GettyImages Europe/GettyImages via AFP ; **41, 3 (hd, 4)** marilyn barbone/AdobeStock ; **42** Designed by starline / Freepik ; **43** Designed by Freepik ; **45 (md)** alenaspl/iStockphoto ; **46 (7,1)** Yellow Dog Productions/GettyImages ; **46 (7,4)** Klaus Vedfelt/GettyImages ; **46 (7,2)** monkeybusinessimages/iStockphoto ; **46 (7,3)** bernardbodo/iStockphoto ; **46 (5d)** uckyo/AdobeStock ; **46 (6)** Designed by Freepik ; **47 (2)** TheresaTibbetts/iStockphoto ; **47 (1)** Designed by Freepik ; **47 (3)** "Merry Christmas, Mr. Bean", 1992, Director: John Birkin Rowan Atkinson with Rowan Atkinson, Collection Christophel © Tiger Television ; **48 (bg)** EMrprize-stock.adobe.com ; **48 (bm)** Alan Dawson/Alamy ; **49 (2hd)** New Africa-stock.adobe.com ; **49 (2hg)** dpa picture alliance archive/Alamy ; **49 (2bm)** izusek/iStockphoto ; **49 (1bg)** Picture Partners-stock.adobe.com ; **49 (1hd)** evgenych-stock.adobe.com ; **49 (1hg)** Martin Lee-stock.adobe.com ; **49 (1hm)** Viktor-stock.adobe.com ; **49 (1bd)** NightandDayImages/iStockphoto ; **49 (1bm)** martinrlee/iStockphoto ; **50, 3 (hd, 5)** sqback/iStockphoto ; **51 (bm)** KeithBishop/GettyImages ; **52 (bg)** Designed by macrovector / Freepik ; **52 (2bm)** Alan Rickman/Warner Bros./Heyday Films © Collection Christophel ; **52 (1bmm)** svetavo-stock.adobe.com ; **52 (1bmg)** CesareFerrari-stock.adobe.com ; **52 (1hmg)** Andrew Twort/Alamy ; **52 (1hg)** A. Pavlov-stock.adobe.com ; **52 (1hd)** lindahughes-stock.adobe.com ; **52 (1bg)** smallblackcat-stock.adobe.com ; **52 (1bd)** Alexandra_K-stock.adobe.com ; **52 (1hmd)** Lidiya-stock.adobe.com ; **52 (2hm)** Tom Felton/Warner Bros./Pictures Heyday Films © Collection Christophel ; **52 (2hd)** "Fantastic Beasts: The Crimes of Grindelwald" by David Yates with Johnny Depp, 2018 ©Heyday Films, Warner Bros./Allstar Picture Library Limited/Alamy ; **52 (1bmd)** benmm/iStockphoto ; **53** Designed by Brgfx / Freepik ; **55 (4hd)** Daniel Radcliffe/Warner Bros. / Heyday Films © Collection Christophel ; **55 (4hmd)** Emma Watson/Warner Bros./Pictures Heyday FilmsEntertainment Pictures/Alamy Stock Photo ; **55 (4hmg)** Michael Gambon/Warner Bros./Pictures Heyday Films/Entertainment Pictures/Entertainment Pictures/Alamy ; **55 (4hg)** Ralph Fiennes/Warner Bros. / Heyday Films © Collection Christophel ; **57 (hd)** Designed by macrovector / Freepik ; **58 (bd)** "The chronicles of Narnia The lion the witch and the wardrobe", 2005, Réal. Andrew Adamson with Tilda Swinton © Walden Media Collection Christophel ; **58 (bm)** "Mistress of Evil", 2019 by Joachim Ronning with Angelina Jolie. Collection ChristopheL © Jaap Buitendijk - Walt Disney Pictures - Roth Films ; **59, 60, 63 (m, b)** redchocolatte/iStockphoto ; **59 (bm)** Designed by macrovector/Freepik ; **59, 3 (hg, 6)** Jozz/Istock ; **61, 62** "Skateboarder Sky Brown's Draw Her Life", A GoldieBlox "Draw My Life Series"/GoldieBlox ; **64 (hg)** PeopleImages/Istock ; **65 (bd)** Designed by macrovector / Freepik ; **68 (m)** Designed by macrovector_official / Freepik ; **68 (2)** photo75/iStockphoto ; **68 (3)** Vladislav Zolotov/iStockphoto ; **68 (1)** A. Astes/Alamy ; **68, 3, 70 (hd, 7)** © P & Co. Ltd./SC 2021 Licencié par Copyrights ; **69 (4)** Inge Johnsson/Alamy Stock Photo ; **69 (5g)** Peter Greenhalgh (UKpix.com)/Alamy ; **69 (5d)** Pictorial Press Ltd/Alamy ; **69 (6)** eye35.pix/Alamy ; **69 (7)** Jon Arnold Images Ldt/Alamy ; **69 (8g)** PA Images/Alamy ; **69 (8d)** Sima Leitner/Shutterstock ; **71** Designed by Nenilkime / Freepik ; **71 (4)** Photocreo Michal Bednarck/Shutterstock ; **71 (1)** robertharding/Alamy ; **71 (2b)** Dmitry Naumov-stock.adobe.com ; **71 (3g)** Daniel Durgan/GettyImages ; **71 (6)** Stefan Kiefer/Image Broker/Photononstop ; **71 (5)** samott-stock.adobe.com ; **71 (2h)** Artur Debat/GettyImages ; **71 (3m)** "The Shard" by Renzo Piano Building Workshopn in collaboration with Adamson Associates (Toronto, Londra)/Panagiotis Kotsovolos/Alamy ; **73 (bd)** Designed by vectorpouch/Freepik ; **74 (2,4)** GoodGnom/iStockphoto ; **74 (2,1)** Misha Shutkevych/iStockphoto ; **74 (2,3)** kosmozoo-iStockphoto ; **74 (2,2)** Tanya St/iStockphoto ; **74 (1hg)** "Creature Comforts", série TV 2003. Collection Christophel © Aardman Animations ; **74 (1hd)** "A Shaun the Sheep Movie: Farmageddon", 2019, by Will Becher and Richard Phelan. Collection Christophel © Aardman Animations - Amazon Prime Video - Anton ; **74 (1bg)** "Wallace and Gromit, the Curse of the Were Rabbit". Real Nick Park and Steve Box. Collection Christophel © Aardman Animations/ DreamWorks Animations ; **74 (3bg)** kebay-stock.adobe.com ; **74 (3hd)** kazy-stock.adobe.com ; **74 (3bmd)** kebay-stock.adobe.com ; **74 (3bmg)** Max Broszat-stock.adobe.com ; **74 (3bd)** Marc-stock.adobe.com ; **74 (3hg)** Marc-stock.adobe.com ; **74 (3m)** Tetra Images, LLC/Alamy ; **75 (2md)** Winnytony/iStockphoto ; **75 (2mg)** simon2579/iStockphoto ; **75 (4,1)** Jaromir Chalabala/Alamy ; **75 (4,2)** Tetra Images, LLC/Alamy ; **75 (4,3)** Adrian Sherratt/Alamy ; **75 (2g)** Sigit Mulyo Utomo/iStockphoto ; **75 (2d)** Felipe Sanchez-stock.adobe.com ; **76 (1,1)** laughingmango/iStockphoto ; **76 (1,2)** Camilla Turriani/Alamy Stock Photo ; **76 (1,3)** Uwe Deffner/Alamy Stock Photo ; **76 (3,1)** Philipp Pound/Alamy ; **76 (3,3)** Mim Friday/Alamy ; **76 (3,2)** Ian Gavan/Getty Images Europe / Getty Images via AFP ; **77 (bhm)** Соседова Анастасия/AdobeStock ; **77 (bbm)** setory/AdobeStock ; **77 (hd)** Romaoslo/Istock ; **77, 3 (m, 8)** akg-images ; **78** "A Day in the Life of a Girl", 1952, Printed by permission of the Norman Rockwell Family Agency Copyright ©1952 the Norman Rockwell Family Entities ; **80** Designed by Freepik ; **81** Edward Hopper, "Cape Cod Evening", 1939, oil on canvas, National Gallery of Art, Washington, DC John Hay Whitney Collection/Adagp, Paris 2021 ; **82** "Mario and Princess Peach" © Marie Pier Marchand ; **83** Collection Christophel © Walt Disney Pictures - Walt Disney Animation Studios ; **84** Norman Rockwell (1894-1978), "The Gossips," 1948. Painting for "The Saturday Evening Post" cover, March 6, 1948. Oil on canvas. Private collection. ©SEPS: Curtis Publishing, Indianapolis, IN.. Printed by permission of the Norman Rockwell Family Agency Copyright ©1948 the Norman Rockwell Family Entities ; **85** Edward Hopper, "Room in New York", 1932 Sheldon Museum of Art, University of Nebraska, Lincoln/Adagp, Paris 2021/Bridgeman Images ; **86 (hd)** © NPS/Rachel Hendrix/https://npgallery.nps.gov/ ; **88 (hg)** Gary Cook/Alamy ; **88 (hd)** RooM the Agency/Alamy ; **88 (bg)** Christoph Lischetzki/Alamy ; **88 (bd)** Lunamarina/iStockphoto ; **88 (hbd, bbd)** albertc111/DigitalVision Vectors/Gettyimages ; **89 (hg)** Tom Stack/Alamy ; **89 (hd)** Tsado-stock.adobe.com ; **89 (hbd)** gusenych/Shutterstock ; **91** John Morris ; **92 (h)** www.nps.gov ; **92 (bd)** Kai Carpenter & Anderson Design Group ; **93 (bg)** Gary Crabbe/Enlightened Images/Alamy ; **94 (2,6)** MicroOne-stock.adobe.com ; **94 (3mm)** dehweh-stock.adobe.com ; **94 (3bd)** Marcos-stock.adobe.com ; **94 (2,3)** dzphotogallery/iStockphoto ; **94 (2,4, 3md)** Svetlana Soloveva/iStockphoto ; **94 (2,2)** alexsko/iStockphoto ; **94 (1g, 1md, 3hm)** Jovanovic Dejan/Shutterstock ; **94 (1mg, 1d, 3bm)** dejanj01/iStockphoto ; **94 (2,1)** jojoo64/iStockphoto ; **94 (2,5)** Rfc1394 ; **95 (3hg)** Ian Dagnall/Alamy ; **95 (3bg)** Westend 61/hemis.fr ; **95 (3md)** David Madison/GettyImages ; **95 (4bg)** Stickers Northwest ; **95 (4bm)** Stickers Northwest ; **95 (4bd)** Decal Dude ; **96, 3 (hd, 10)** George Rinhart/GettyImages ; **96 (mg)** Heritage Images/GettyImages ; **96 (bd)** Popperfoto/GettyImages ; **97 (hg)** Buyenlarge/GettyImages ; **97 (md)** Alfred Eisenstaedt/GettyImages ; **97 (bg)** Bettmann/GettyImages ; **98 (hg)** DE AGOSTINI PICTURE LIBRARY/GettyImages ; **98 (mg)** General Photographic Agency/GettyImages ; **98 (bg)** Bettmann/GettyImages ; **99, 100** From teacher.scholastic.com. Copyright by Scholastic Inc. Reprinted by permission of Scholastic Inc. ; **101 (2g)** YummyBuum/AdobeStock ; **101 (2d)** kadirkaba/IStock ; **101 (5hg, hm)** Ariel Skelley/GettyImages ; **101 (hd)** Victor Coscaron/EyeEm/GettyImages ; **101 (mg, bd)** Tetra Images/GettyImages ; **101 (mm, md)** Fatcamera/GettyImages ; **102 (hm)** FrankRamspott/Istock ; **102 (m)** Designed by macrovector/Freepik ; **103 (5,1,2,3)** fonikum/Istock ; **103 (5,4,5)** ambo182/Istock ; **103 (5,6)** Enis Aksoy/Istock ; **104** Designed by Harryarts / Freepik ; **105 (1g)** Danny Lehman/The Image Bank/Gettyimages ; **105 (1d)** Frederick Millett / Alamy ; **105 (2g)** Orlando/Hulton Archive/Gettyimages ; **105 (2d)** Chu-Wen Lin / Alamy ; **105 (2m)** Archive Holdings Inc./The Image Bank/Gettyimages ; **109 (bd)** Gelpi/AdobeStock ; **111 (hd)** Diary of Wimpy Kid "Wimpy Kid Do-It-Yourself Book" by Jeff Kinney (first published in the US by Harry N Abrams, 2008, Puffin Books 2008) © Jeff Kinney, 2008. Wimpy kid text and illustrations copyright © 2008, 2011 Wimpy kid, Inc. "Diary of a Wimpy kid" and Greg Heffey cover images are tradermarks if Wimpy Kid, Inc. Book design by Jeff Kinney and Chad W. Beckerman. Cover photograph by Geof Spear, colouring on last sixteen colour comics by Nate Greenwall. All rights reserved ; **115** copyright Text and Ilustration © Liz Pichon, 2011, 2013 The right of Liz Pichon to be identified as the author of this work has been asserted by her ; **117 (hd)** inarik-stock.adobe.com ; **121 (md)** "13-Year-Old FEARLESS Surfing Prodigy", Kai Williams/Whistle ; **123 (md)** Winnytony/iStockphoto ; **125 (hd)** "Minion Gothic Art Print" Le Duc ; **127 (bhm)** T. Michel/AdobeStock ; **127 (bbm)** jusep/AdobeStock ; **139 (g)** © P & Co. Ltd./SC 2021 Licencié par Copyrights.

Références des textes ; 10 "Hello Goodbye" (John Lennon / Paul McCartney) © Sony/ATV Tunes LLC, 1967. Avec l'aimable autorisation de Sony Music Publishing (France). Droits protégés. ; **19** From "Revenge of the Lunch Ladies" by Kenn Nesbitt, copyright © 2007. Reprinted by Permission of Meadowbrook Acquired, an imprint of Hachette Book Group, Inc. ; **26** "The One who Invented Trick or Treat" from "Every Thing On It" by Shel Silverstein. © 2011 Evil Eye, LLC. By permission of Edite Kroll Literary Agency Inc. ; **50** Copyright © The Roald Dahl Story Company Ltd/Quentin Blake, 1983, 1984, 2020/Puffin Books/Penguin Random House Children's, UK ; **92** www.nps.gov ; **99** From teacher.scholastic.com. Copyright by Scholastic Inc. Reprinted by permission of Scholastic Inc.

Nous remercions chaleureusement Noah Bahe, River D'Costa-Stephenson, Louis Dupin, Grace Flannery, Mai-Lihn et Emilie Grabiel, Emily Martha et Laura Green, Martin Harragin, Matilda Moore-Evans, Harry Morris, Neve O'Leary, Ruby Sprinkle.